Suicide and Young People

Also by Arnold Madison

Vigilantism in America
Vandalism: The Not-So-Senseless Crime

SUICIDE
and Young People

Arnold Madison

CLARION BOOKS
TICKNOR & FIELDS : A HOUGHTON MIFFLIN COMPANY
NEW YORK

For my sister Barbara,
who gave me my first dictionary

Clarion Books
Ticknor & Fields, a Houghton Mifflin Company

Library of Congress Cataloging in Publication Data
Madison, Arnold.   Suicide and young people.
"A Clarion book."
Bibliography
Includes index.
Summary: Discusses possible causes for the
rising rate of suicide among young people.
1. Youth—Suicidal behavior—Juvenile
literature.   2. Suicide—Prevention—Juvenile
literature.   [1. Suicide]   I. Title.
HV6546.M24   616.8′5844   77-13240
ISBN 0-395-28913-0
Paperback ISBN 0-395-30011-8

(Previously published by The Seabury Press
under ISBN 0-8164-3211-2)

V   10   9   8   7   6   5

Contents

Acknowledgments

The people I most want to thank, unfortunately, cannot be named in print in order to preserve their anonymity. These are the persons who willingly allowed themselves to be interviewed concerning their own suicide attempts or the suicides of friends or relatives. The interviewees were at all times honest and probed some sensitive emotions in the hope that this book would help other people through periods of emotional stress. All the case histories described in this book are true, and only the names and occasionally the locations have been changed.

The author would also like to thank the high school students who filled out the questionaires on their personal feelings about suicide. Neither the students nor the high school can be named because the school authorities are afraid of negative parental reaction if the members of the community learned that topics like suicide were discussed in the health and sociology classes. Tragically, the youngsters are more aware of the problem of suicide among young people than their parents.

There are individuals who can be and should be named. These people helped me to locate research material or to meet persons who had attempted suicide. Though their names will be grouped together, each person was invaluable and contributed greatly to this book.

My warmest thanks are offered to:

> Pauline C. Bartel
> Nancy Connell
> David Lee Drotar
> Dorothy Brenner Francis
> Willard A. Heaps
> Tess Langworthy
> Donald E. Mack
> Judy Madison
> Shirley Morgan
> Joan Lowery Nixon
> Eileen Siegal
> Phyllis A. Whitney
> Lee Wyndham

And, finally, I am indebted to the staff and volunteers of San Francisco Suicide Prevention, Inc. All members connected with that organization were extra helpful during my visit to their offices and revealed themselves to be sincere, dedicated workers in the fight against suicide.

A.M.

". . . human life is unique,
cannot be recovered and has to be
saved at almost any cost."

Dr. Uri Lowental
The New York Times   October 26, 1975

1

Why?

In the nine-day period from February 21 to March 1, 1976, three headlines appeared in New York State newspapers.

"Austrian At Union [College] Is Suicide
—*Schenectady Gazette*

"Harris Death Ruled Suicide"
—*The Saratogian*

"Boy, 14, Shoots Self: Motive Unknown"
—*Newsday*

At first appearance, New York state might seem to have been in the midst of a suicide epidemic. This was not the case, however. At least not any more so than the rest of the nation. The three victims were further proof that youthful suicides have increased 92% in the last several years in the United States. On the international level, the World Health Organization (WHO) at a special 1974 conference in Luxembourg stated that suicides for the age group from fifteen through college age had risen 100%. The three young men mentioned above, however, were not merely numbers in a percentage figure. Each had been a human being with goals and dreams.

The two roommates of Chris B., 26, arrived home late one night in Schenectady to find a note in their room, directing them to the attic of the big, old apartment house. There, they found Chris had slashed his wrists and temples and then hung himself. Chris, a citizen of Austria, was due to graduate in two weeks from Union College and return to his native country. His two friends were shocked by his death and unable to give any reason for their roommate's suicide.

Twenty-two miles away from Union College is Saratoga Springs. Soon after Chris B.'s death, a February morning seemed to promise a mild day. Though the sun would not rise for another one hundred and twelve minutes, the temperature was already in the low thirties and the sky cloudless as Robert Harris opened his garage door at 5:15 A.M., preparing to drive to work. Inside, he discovered his son Ted, 19, had hung himself. Mr. Harris immediately cut the body free and tried to revive Ted, but the boy was already dead. No notes were found, and the family told the police that Ted had seemed in high spirits the day before. Later the Saratoga County Coroner ruled out any possibility of foul play.

Friday, February 27, was Eddie J.'s fourteenth birthday. His father had given him new bowling equipment as a gift, so early the next evening Eddie, his father, and Jim, a seventeen-year-old brother, went bowling as they did every weekend. After returning to their home on Long Island, the parents went to inspect an air-conditioner that was on sale, leaving the two boys alone. Between seven and eight o'clock, Jim was working in the attached garage when Eddie deliberately locked the connecting door between the garage and the house. The older boy finally managed to get out. When he entered the house, he spotted Eddie at the top of the stairway, holding a .38 caliber revolver.

"Tell Mom and Dad I love them, and I love you." After saying that, Eddie pulled the trigger, killing himself with a single shot.

The Suffolk County police said there was no permit for the gun, which apparently had been in the parents' upstairs bedroom. Nor was there any clue to Eddie's reason for suicide.

Psychologists have characterized the life history of a suicide as usually including a series of failures, sometimes alcoholism or other drug-related addictions and almost always disordered interpersonal relationships. Except in the case of Ted Harris, none of these conditions seemed evident in the three boys' lives.

The two roommates of Chris B. said the Austrian student had been successful academically and socially, and the only unpleasantness, if that is the word, in his life was that he would be leaving his American friends when he returned to Austria. But this was only a minor thread in the whole fabric of Chris B.'s life.

Ted Harris had quit high school a week and a half before his suicide, but his life was not a failure. A job was in the offing, and his close friends scoffed at the possibility of drug addiction. Neither his companions nor family had seen any indication that Ted believed his life had reached a point where nothing positive lay ahead.

The death of Eddie J. is even more puzzling because, on the surface, he seemed to have a fuller and more rewarding life than many boys his age. His family was a close one and were all well liked by their neighbors. Eddie tutored other children in his middle class black neighborhood who needed help in math and English and had recently told his father that he wanted to become a teacher.

A neighbor who resided near the family said, "I wished him a happy birthday Friday, and he gave me a hug and a kiss and told me about some [record] albums he was going to buy with the money relatives had given him for his birthday."

The assistant principal of the school where Eddie was in the eighth grade described the boy as a good student who was active in school programs and seemed to have many friends. "He was a very, very nice kid, who was quiet but not despondent. It just doesn't make sense."

Although youthful suicides such as Chris, Ted, and Eddie make no sense to the grieving survivors, suicide must have seemed the only viable course of action for the victim. Some situation or series of psychological blows drove them to use their intelligence and power to destroy that very intelligence and power.

Consider the case of Larry G., an attempted suicide that never made the newspapers. Larry was nineteen years old at the time, came from a middle-income family, and had managed to get through high school with grades which even he called "pretty bad." He was living at home and had recently purchased a used car for which his father had lent him the money.

"Everything that happened that night was my fault," Larry said. "Art didn't want to go drinking, but I told him, 'C'mon, we'll just have a few beers.' That was about nine [o'clock], I guess. Something like that. We sat at a table in the back of this crummy bar and kept ordering pitchers [of beer].

"Artie kept wanting to leave, but I'd get us more [beer]. About one [o'clock] we were pretty smashed. I mean really smashed. We left and got about four blocks away. Wham! I was driving and really slow. But the car I hit got messed up. Mine, too. I went right across the road into this parked car.

"And listen to this. It was almost right in front of the police station. No shit. I'm not kidding. Art's head hit the windshield. I guess I hit the mirror because it [my head] was bleeding. This old bitch come running out of the bowling alley, screaming like hell.

"The police gave me a couple of tickets and brought me and Art to the hospital. That's when it came to me. We were sitting there—waiting for the doctor and making jokes—and I suddenly knew I was going to kill myself."

"They sewed up my head, and I asked the doctor, 'Is it okay for me to go home?' You see, I didn't want to stay. I wanted to get home and get on with it. You can't imagine . . . you really can't imagine how cool it [the planned suicide] made me feel inside."

The doctor did not keep Larry and Art in the hospital. Arthur's parents arrived soon to take him home. Larry lived a few blocks away, and even though Art's parents offered to drive him, he said he would walk.

"And I looked around at those streets. And, man, I didn't feel sorry to be getting out of there [killing himself] at all. Not one bit. I got home. My parents were gone for the weekend. I put some Neil Diamond on, got my father's Scotch and a razor blade.

"I remember this so clearly. I mean it could've been yesterday. Diamond was singing "Solitary Man" and I was thinking, 'You're right, man. You are so right.' I had really screwed up everything. I was sure I'd lose my license and the insurance company would drop me. I couldn't drive. But I had to drive to my job, so I'd probably lose that."

When asked if he thought how his parents would feel, Larry replied, "I knew they'd be upset at first. But also I thought they'd be better off without me. Maybe even happier. So I began cutting my wrists— on the top and the bottom [of the wrists]—and drinking booze. I guess I'm a better drinker [than suicide-attempter]. I guess I crawled into bed.

"And you know? This is crazy. I woke up the next morning and thought I just had too much to drink with Artie. And then I saw my wrists. Oh, shit, man!"

Except for Larry who discussed his suicide attempt with an interviewer, the other three suicides mentioned in this chapter left no notes behind. But there have been young suicides and attempted suicides who have been able to explain in part what brought them to the point of self-destruction. In a majority of cases, the problem cited was *not* insurmountable, help was available, and in many cases, friends and family had failed to recognize the warning signals of intended suicide.

Suicide is now considered a major U.S. public health problem. This book will investigate the causes, seeking answers for those who call for help. Suicide—that act which the victim knows will result in death—is, after all, a last desperate cry for help.

2

Two Views
Since the Beginning

Though certain animals display what appear to be self-destructive characteristics, suicide came with the appearance of human beings on earth. Since the earliest recorded history, suicide has had its foes and advocates.

Organized religions were the first to condemn self-death. Christianity holds life to be a gift from God, and therefore only God may take life away. Also, a suicide was in violation of the Fifth Commandment delivered to Moses on Sinai: Thou shalt not kill. In A.D. 563, the Christian Council of Braga stipulated penalties for suicides by prohibiting ". . . commemoration at the oblation. Nor shall they be brought to be buried with psalms." The Judeo-Christian tradition as well as Islam held that suicide in the form of martyrdom was permissible, however. The Jews also contended that suicide was a positive action if employed to prevent torture, rape, or slavery. King Saul fell on his sword after defeat in battle. The mass suicide of the defenders of Masada, a Jewish fortress beseiged by the Romans in A.D. 72–73, to prevent capture was considered an heroic climax to their struggle.

The ancient Greeks also adopted a double view toward suicide. To avoid disgrace, the single Spartan soldier who survived the Battle of Thermopylae killed himself, thereby gaining popular approval. Generally, however, suicide was labeled shameful. In Athens, the body of a suicide was buried outside the city, and the hand that ended his life was cut off and buried elsewhere. The Pythagoreans in ancient Greece saw life as a penitential journey in which a person's humility and submission were an indication of his value. Thus, a suicide revealed that an individual was worthless. Aristotle spoke of suicide as being uncourageous. Plato supported this philosophy, though he specified sickness or debilitation as honorable reasons for a self-inflicted death.

Incurable illness and the infirmity of old age were acceptable reasons to the Roman Stoics also, although the Roman government imposed penalties upon certain types of suicides. For instance, if a slave committed suicide, his body was disposed of like refuse, and his owner, if the death occurred within a few months of purchase, could demand the return of the purchase money.

Emperor Hadrian equated a soldier's suicide to

desertion because the man's death weakened Rome's power against her enemies. The soldier's name would be officially dishonored, and the customary funeral rites were denied. In addition, his personal property was forfeited, either to the State or to the legion in which he had served. The only exception would be if the soldier was judged insane at the time of his death.

The third category of illegal suicide in Rome was that of a citizen under criminal indictment. Apparently, such a death deprived the state of exacting its punishment so this class of victim suffered the same penalty as was imposed upon the soldier. Again, there was a qualification in the law. If the individual was later proven innocent of the crime, there would be no takeover by the state of the person's belongings.

Strangely, there was no legal prohibition against suicide by the ordinary Roman citizen. During the Middle Ages, however, other European nations punished *all* suicides usually through degradations inflicted upon the body. In Danzig, a Northern European city, a suicide's remains were not allowed to be carried through the outer door of the building in which that person had died. The body was lifted through a window and lowered to the street by pulleys. The window frame would then be burned. In France, the body might be burned, dragged through the streets, or thrown on the public garbage heap.

In Brittany, however, even as late as the seventeenth century, certain French Christian sects permitted suicide by a person with an incurable disease. The sufferer became an indirect suicide by appealing for "The Holy Stone." The family of the invalid would gather, and a religious rite would be performed. The oldest living relative would then drop a heavy stone on the person's head, ending his or her life. This was an isolated custom, however, on a continent that generally viewed suicide as evil.

At this same time England was employing similar methods to those used in other European nations to discourage suicide. The early English names for suicide convey the emotional value attached to the deed. "Self-homicide" and "self-murder" were in common usage, and like a murderer, the suicide's body was often hung from a gibbet or buried at a crossroads with a stake driven through the heart. Though Edward Phillips' book, *New Worlds of Words,* contained the first written use of the word "suicide" in 1662, the law condemning suicide remained on the books until the early nineteenth century using the phrase "one who commits murder upon himself." The last recorded burial at a crossroads took place in Chelsea, when a Londoner committed suicide in 1823. A suicide's property, however, continued to be seized by the Crown until 1870.

Not all societies reflected this negative philosophy of suicide. Certain Eskimo civilizations practiced suicide motivated by social concern. These peoples existed in regions where the food supply was limited so, at times, aged members of the group would purposely wander off and freeze to death, in order that the others might sustain themselves with whatever food was available. In Japan, suicide has been an integral part of the moral code since the days of the Samurai warrior. The only honorable means for a disgraced warrior to redeem himself would be to commit hara-kiri or *seppuku,* in which he disemboweled himself with his own sword.

Honorable self-death has never received wide public approval in the United States for several reasons. The pioneer spirit held as one of its tenets that the struggle to overcome obstacles and troubles was courageous. Therefore suicide was cowardly. Also a majority of early American settlers followed the Judeo-Christian tradition, which to this day regards suicide as sinful. Other historical stands on the question of suicide are present in modern America.

Early American law, basically derived from British law, reflected the mother country's attitude toward suicide. Unsuccessful suicides faced either prosecution or institutionalization as insane. Today, only nine states list suicide as a crime, but law enforcement agencies rarely prosecute attempted suicide, though it is still legally a misdeameanor or a felony. Some states enforce their laws by requiring mandatory hospitalization to protect the person from further self-harm. Eighteen states, including New York, Wisconsin, and California, have no existing law prohibiting suicide, though it is a crime to encourage or aid in another person's suicide. In addition, twenty states have no penal statute referring to suicide.

Present-day suicides do sometimes face economic

punishment. Insurance companies generally specify a waiting period of from one to two years after a policy's incipience before the company is required to make payments to the surviving friends or relatives of an insured suicide. Some companies refuse any benefits if the insured has committed suicide.

The Aristotelian philosophy that suicide is cowardly resembles the nineteenth century American belief that suicide is "the coward's way out." Doctors today are frequently begged not to list suicide as the cause when filling out the official death certificate because the survivors want to be spared "the disgrace." Moreover, medical people are caught in the middle of the conflict about suicide. Occasionally, the attending physician of a person dying from a terminal disease is asked for a prescription for pain-killing drugs in sufficient quantity so the patient may end his or her suffering forever.

These requests are merely a desire for a more sophisticated form of the Holy Stone as are the half-million "living wills," which the Euthanasia Society of America has distributed since 1969. These documents are signed statements by people in good health who indicate that, should they develop a terminal disease, they have no desire to be kept alive by mechanical means.

"People are more and more frightened by medical advances that just keep people alive," said Mrs. Elizabeth Halsey, executive director of the Society. "People who are very old or very ill prefer to die quietly and peacefully at home."

More evidence of contrasting American opinions on suicide could be noted in the April 1975 Gallup Poll, which based its finding upon interviews with 1,535 people in 300 localities. Three questions were posed about a person's moral right to end his or her life in three situations:

(1) when that person was an extremely heavy burden on the family;
(2) when a person experienced great pain with no hope of improvement;
(3) when a person had an incurable disease.

Little difference was noted between the answers of men and women, but the survey found divergent beliefs depending upon the interviewee's age. Fewer than 30% of the people who were between the age of eighteen and twenty-nine, both with and without college educations, said a person had the right to terminate his or her life when that individual was a heavy burden to the family. More than half of the same group believed a person had the moral right to terminate his or her life if suffering great pain and terminal illness.

Taking the entire count, however, which included replies by young and old Americans, the majority opinion changes. According to the complete pool, 53% of all those interviewed thought an individual did *not* have the moral right to end his or her life when suffering from an incurable disease. Only 40% believed such a person did have the right.

Despite this general anti-suicide point of view, even today certain suicidal acts still have positive values as they have all through history. Soldiers who refuse to retreat or surrender in the face of certain death are regarded as heroes and not suicides. Religious devotees, who will not renounce their faith and therefore die, earn people's respect and are honored as religious martyrs. People who resist torture designed to make them reveal secrets entrusted to them, or who choose death willingly, such as the secret agents who carry a suicide pill, are considered great patriots.

But at no time in history has a youthful suicide, unless it fell into one of the above categories, ever received approval, and at no time in history has the problem of youthful suicides ever been so widespread as it is now. People are shocked and saddened by a young person killing him- or herself. The feeling goes beyond religious or philosophical beliefs. No matter how severe the victim's problem, people are certain that a young person has the years and the capabilities to deal with the situation and maneuver his or her life back onto a successful track.

The fact remains, however, that increasing numbers of young people cannot or will not sustain themselves and thereby choose self-destruction.

3

Suicide and Young People

The figures are frightening. During the years 1945–1969, 4.9% per population of 100,000 were youthful suicides in the United States. In 1970–1972, the rate had almost doubled to 9.2% per 100,000, while the national overall rate of suicide had only increased 0.7%. Youthful suicide is now the second highest killer of people between the ages of ten and twenty-four. The first ranking cause is automobile accidents, and authorities are certain some of these may be suicidal. However, the official death certificate used in most states can only be marked suicide when there is no doubt, as in the suicide of Gary C.

On August 3, 1976, eighteen-year-old Gary C. was driving his late-model Duster west along the New York Thruway near Amsterdam, New York. Suddenly, purposefully, he veered around the divider and drove west in the eastbound lane. Several cars swerved into the ditch to avoid the rapidly accelerating car. Finally, a tractor trailer that could not escape the oncoming car was struck. All that remained of the Duster was a charred, twisted hulk, welded to the truck's cab by the accident-caused fire. Miraculously, the truck driver sustained only minor injuries. Identification of Gary's body had to be established through his dental records.

Friends of Gary acknowledged the fact that recently he had a serious argument with his girlfriend, and the couple had parted. Gary had been upset when there seemed no possible way to be reunited with the girl.

On the surface this suicide appears to be a matter of momentary overreaction to a temporary problem. That certainly is the cause of some youthful suicides. The teenage years are recognized by mental health experts as a time of sharp and rapid emotional ups-and-downs. During these emotional bouts, a young person may make a hasty decision, such as running away or suicide, without considering the full impact of the action.

"It's shocking, but young people often look on it [suicide] as a temporary way out," said Ms. Nancy H. Allen, former president of the American Association of Suicidology.

March, 1976: A young man in Pueblo, Colorado, shoots himself in the head with a .44 caliber revolver. The reason: A heated argument with his father about whether or not the boy could make a weekend trip with friends.

April 1976: A twenty-year-old youth hangs himself

in a Yonkers, New York, jail cell hours after his arrest. The reason: He thought he had been arrested for a former crime. He did not know that he had been apprehended on a warrant that was worthless. The matter would have been cleared up in a few hours.

February 1977: A thirteen-year-old girl in Glendale, California, fires a .38 caliber bullet through her brain. The reason: Her favorite television actor had killed himself a few days before. Her suicide note stated that she did not want to live in the world without him.

Momentary and total depression is not the sole motivation for youthful suicides as many people mistakenly think. In fact, it may be one of the least important influences. The problem is chameleonlike, and oversimplification hides the numerous causes that are discovered as more case histories are explored. There are numerous professional theories about the causes of suicide and the way the problem should be studied. Some experts feel that investigations made with survivors of suicide attempts and those who almost attempted suicide are invalid. There is a difference, they claim, between the successful suicide and the attempter. The most telling evidence would be revealed by the successful suicide. Obviously, that source of information is lost forever.

Most experts do agree, however, that the "wounding" theory is a major cause. Psychological wounding, generally during the very young years, causes the loss of a sense of competence. Once destroyed, the sense of competence can rarely be regained. A dominant characteristic of the personalities of a majority of youthful suicides is this feeling of an inability to solve problems.

Ironically, many people who lack this inner belief grow up to become very capable people. Their success comes from a constant struggle to succeed so that they will, in some way, achieve this sense of competence. They are doomed to strive for a lifetime to prove to themselves that they are capable and, in most cases, will never truly believe that they are.

This self-image of incompetence generates, in some people, an unassuageable hunger for love. "Love me," they beg. And when love is given, they need more proof and more proof. Unreasonable demands are made upon the lovers, relatives, and friends of such people to prove the unprovable. Often these others cannot supply what is demanded. The person then feels frustrated in his or her search for love. Out of this frustration comes a rage against those who appear to refuse the demands. Yet the person who is bursting with rage cannot leave the relationship, causing a further assault on this individual's competence.

Some suicide experts suggest this as a possible cause of actor Freddie Prinze's suicide in January 1977. If Prinze was a person who had never developed an internal feeling of competence, the cause was not his family, which was a warm, loving one. Growing up a Spanish-American in Harlem, however, might well have created a feeling of rejection by society. Rejection in the very young years, whether it be by parents or society, can destroy the sense of competence.

"I never knew someone that had so many fantasies," a friend of Prinze's said about their boyhood days on West 157th Street.

Another facet of Prinze's mental makeup was revealed when an old-time pal related an incident from those early years. "Freddie would never fight. One time a kid lots shorter than Freddie hit him over the head with a baseball bat so hard the bat broke. Then he got Freddie to buy him a new one."

Freddie Prinze's fantasies continued as he matured, but now they were played out before television audiences. As a young boy, he dreamed of a magical future; as an adult, he created a youth he never lived. Fans knew the line about roaches in his apartment building being so big they used to eat at the dinner table, and the joke that his Puerto Rican mother met his Hungarian father on the subway when the two of them were picking each other's pockets. He purposely portrayed himself as a tough kid who grew up on enchiladas and carried a switchblade knife. This was a totally inaccurate picture but good comedy material and, perhaps, wishful thinking. After all, tough kids grow up to be tough adults.

What happens to a person when he discovers that the greatest of all fantasies—the American myth of fame and fortune—does not bring the fabled happiness or the belief that you can overcome the latest problem? Friends and business associates of Prinze's told authorities that Freddie was despondent about the breakup of his marriage, which may have been caused by a desire for too much love. The prospect of finding happiness without his wife and child seemed impossible. In other words, Freddie Prinze did not feel confident that he could handle his problems.

The loss of the sense of competence can occur in the home, too. Some people have been emotionally crippled through outright parental rejection, but more often disparagement, which can be insidiously destructive, is the culprit.

Cathy H. is twenty-three years old, a highly trained person who is the private secretary for a medical specialist. Six years ago she attempted suicide with an overdose of sleeping pills. Her older brother rushed her to a hospital before the pills could take effect. The immediate cause for the suicide attempt was school.

"I had no idea of where I was going academically," Cathy says. "My grades dropped. School was a sick joke for me. Classes bored me. They seemed ridiculous. I spoke in class just to talk—and to avoid being thought of as quiet, as I had been the previous year in school. I got violently depressed often, and frequently stayed out of school because of it. . . . I had no close friends."

The long-term problem, as Cathy herself now realizes, is that she was never allowed to develop a sense of competence. Recalling her young years,

Cathy says of her parents: "My father looks like a prune and is about as responsive. Two out of three times he won't answer if you ask him a question. The third time, he will give you an irate answer, which means, in effect, shut up and mind your own beeswax. Yet, he mutters on and on about the importance of 'having a dialogue' and 'relating to people.'

"My mother is one of the many unemployed Ph.D.'s in New York. She loves to dictate opinions to me and loves even more to ridicule me for opinions I have that aren't hers. She has a low opinion of my artwork and lets me know. She thinks my mind is mediocre and that I should learn to face it. She won't touch my emotional life. Once I tried to tell her about my problems with a boy friend, and she said, 'Why don't you do something more interesting. Like watch Watergate.' "

There is another type of parental rejection less direct than that Cathy suffered, but widespread. Many youngsters are growing up today knowing that their mothers and fathers do not enjoy them as people. A joyless sense of duty is transmitted to the child by parents who view children as merely another responsibility: a living, monthly mortgage payment.

Other parents attempt to use a child as a weapon against the marriage partner. This can have a devastating psychological effect on a youngster of any age. Often the actual rivalry between the parents has been sublimated for years, but the growing child senses the underlying tensions. Even if the home has been a pleasant environment, and the marriage does not begin to deteriorate until the child has reached his or her teenage years, the results can be traumatic. Consider what happened to Grace L.

"When I grew up, I considered that I had a good family life, which is why when things started falling apart, it hit me. It was just something that had been very nice and then it was gone, and I could feel it going. I can remember when the arguments changed, the tone of voices that were being used, the feelings that were being expressed."

Apparently, Grace's parents were aware that things were falling apart, too. For then came the period of time when she was used as an "emotional volleyball."

"My father was the one who put pressure on me. I had to be on his side. So I'd get a love note from him. But one day there I was telling him he wasn't right. Then I'd get a hate note from him. He went out, when I was seventeen years old, to enlist me as a recruit. He was laying these heavy things on me. I'm sorry, but a girl of sixteen or seventeen should never hear the intimacies of his marriage, stuff like that, all designed to get me on his side. And for a while he had me because I was so desperate for some kind of a rationale, for some kind of reason, that I would accept anything. Anything.

"I started to pull away from him, and he didn't make it easy. But at that point I was getting a lot of pressure and I wanted to ease out of my relationship with him because it was a pretty destructive relationship."

The effect of this turmoil upon Grace?

"For a long time I couldn't remember a day when I didn't think about doing myself in. And some days were worse than others. Some days it was just a constant thing from the minute I got up. And other days it was something that would run through your mind."

The constant dwelling upon the idea of suicide caused her to become a collector. "I can remember sitting in the bathroom and getting out a razor blade and looking at it. Also one day I went into the medicine cabinet and got out a bottle of pills. And I thought about that, too. Kind of like filed things away."

The effect of rejection upon a child, subtle or overt, causes some youngsters to withdraw from life. Rather than feeling the pain, they try to blot out their frustration and misery by avoiding any situation or relationship where their emotions may be touched. Frequently, these people, who have found deadness as their only security through life, view suicide as the ultimate numbness.

There are several other ideas that may motivate youthful suicides and help justify their actions to themselves. One is what an expert has termed the "Romeo and Juliet Factor." The romantic tradition fostered in fiction and drama of dying for love appeals to the idealistic young person. Research has shown that romantic difficulties have been the major cause of suicide attempts among college students. Female students often made attempts that were not serious but were designed to revive a weakening relationship. The number of male college students who attempted suicide over women was rare. Depression resulting from the loss of a male lover was more frequently a cause of the suicide attempt. Suicidal male students usually were not afflicted with guilt about their homosexuality. The dominant factor behind the attempt was rejection by another male during the homosexual relationship.

Another basic belief held by many young people is that a person should have complete control over his or her life. After all, they say, we make decisions about our lives all the time. The choice to die is therefore a person's right.

"If you have a job that is a downer, you quit," said twenty-year-old Bill R. "And if you have a life that is a downer, you can quit that, too."

The argument against this philosophy is that you can usually find another job, but there is no chance for another life. Whether you agree that a person's rights extend to the point of taking his or her own life is unimportant. There is a subculture in the United States that adheres to this belief. Some of its members have become suicide statistics.

There is one other widespread cause of youthful suicides: adult blindness.

Perhaps a false stereotype of teenagers has contributed to their blindness, or possibly the demands of their lives make them underestimate the importance of a young person's problems.

Mike B. is a tall, slim fourteen-year-old from New

Jersey. Six months ago he tried to kill himself by asphyxiation in the family car. He was asked why he hadn't talked his problems over with his family. His mother and father seemed like concerned parents. Wouldn't they have listened?

"Oh, they would have listened all right. You know what my father once said to me. 'Teenagers are always moody. You're supposed to be unhappy. Later, when you look back, you'll see it was the happiest time of your life.' *Supposed* to be unhappy? What kind of weird thinking is that?"

Whether it is a lack of appreciation of a young person's very real anxieties or one of the many other causes, the problem of youthful suicides is growing today and robbing the nation of its most important natural resource: human life.

4

Youthful Suicide
and the Minorities

Webster's New Collegiate Dictionary offers the following as one definition of a minority: "A part of a population differing from others in some characteristics and often subjected to differential treatment."

Unless the "differential treatment" is positive—providing more to the person rather than depriving him or her of something—the effect is to block a sense of fulfillment, and the result is usually despair. Therefore, by definition alone, we might well expect the suicide rates for minority groups in the United States to be greater than those for other sectors of the population, considering the fact that suicide is often precipitated by a feeling of rejection.

Investigating one minority group, women, we find that more females attempt suicide than men; eight out of ten attempts are by women. The rates of successful suicide do not reflect this fact because women tend to succeed less often than men since they usually try less lethal methods. Women generally use barbiturates; men, guns.

In a recent ten-year period in California, the actual rate of successful suicides among women increased. The same situation was reflected in nationwide statistics also. The California ratio between male and female suicides has changed from about three men to one woman in 1960 to 1.7 males to one female in 1970. This indicates an increase of more than forty percent.

San Francisco shows a slightly different trend than the rest of California. Recently, Mr. Roger Cornut, Executive Director of San Francisco Suicide Prevention, Inc., discussed the male-female suicide difference.

"In the past ten years, gradually there was a greater number of female suicides in San Francisco. Until a point about four years ago when approximately fifty per cent of all suicides were committed by women. But now, in the last three or four years, gradually we are coming back to a large number of males and fewer females."

When asked why there was an increased rate of successful female suicides during those particular years, Mr. Cornut theorized: "As the Women's Liberation Movement took shape, more and more women felt they *had* to perform roles of responsibilities in their lives. We all know that not everyone is ready to handle stress. And, as there was more

stress, there were more emotional disturbances leading to drinking and suicide."

That may account for the rise in the female suicide rate. But why the decline during the last several
years in San Francisco?

"As women get into trouble—emotionally speaking—they are more prone to seek help for it. Generally, when a man has emotional problems, he's more
prone to rationalize—blame his boss or his wife —or
seek morbid outlets such as drinking or a sportive
gal—other things than saying, 'I have a problem. I
need help.'

"So maybe as more women were getting into
trouble, more of them started to seek and obtain
help."

Roger Cornut, however, is the first to admit these
are his personal deductions. The subject of why
more woman attempt suicide than men and the reasons for the recent fluctuation in their success pattern have never been fully explored in a scientific
study. We know that great sociological changes can
affect the suicide rate, as we also know that the roots
of suicide are firmly implanted in the culture where
it occurs. Possibly the badly needed research about
women and suicide that is getting under way will
unearth some answers.

The same lack of scientific data holds true for the
causes of suicide among other American minorities.
". . . we have a national increase of suicides among
young people in general, most pronounced among
nonwhite youth. It could even be called an epidemic

because it exceeds normal expectations based upon past experience." Thus wrote Richard H. Seiden in the "Public Affairs Report" of August 1974.

This statement is substantiated by the high black suicide rates, particularly in urban areas. But when researchers try to investigate the statistics covering suicide among Spanish-Americans, they find that much of this data is classified only under white or nonwhite. Whether the Hispanic suicides in the United States are placed under the white or the nonwhite label seems to be determined by the social background and location of the individual charged with this duty rather than by legal definitions.

In the early 1970s, there were nearly nine million Spanish-Americans in this country, including Puerto Ricans, Mexicans, and other Latin Americans. About one-fourth of these people lived below the poverty level, a problem which would certainly be reflected in the suicide rate. Other stresses burdened their lives, too. Hispanic persons tend to complete less schooling than either blacks or other whites. Bilingual home environments often impede their scholastic progress. The chances for upward mobility are hampered by social, economic, and prejudicial factors. Some youngsters of this minority might well opt for self-destruction rather than a lifetime plagued with disappointment.

Juan S. lived in a town one hundred miles from Des Moines, Iowa. For the last several months, his parents had noticed a dramatic change in their sixteen-year-old son. He had let his hair grow longer, and his clothes had become sloppier. Many teenagers go through this transformation, but there were other signs that the boy's inner turmoil was more serious. He was using drugs and cutting classes at the high school where he was a sophomore. Then a pending charge of marijuana-smoking caused Juan to run away. The boy took a checkbook with him and passed several bad checks before the police apprehended him as a runaway.

Placed in a county jail cell, Juan sat staring at the small, rusted sink and the dripping toilet bowl and the small bed with the gray and white striped mattress. The hearing about his marijuana-smoking charge was to be held in twenty-two days, and Juan was certain he would be sent to a nearby training school for boys. This would be one more blow in a life of unhappiness.

His father and another relative visited him the first night. Later Juan's father said, "I think he was high on something. I think it was a combination of liquor and drugs."

On the afternoon of the third day, Juan penciled a message on the cement wall:

> I want to die. No dope. No O.D. No rope. No hang. Razor blade. I cut my wrist. No blood. I aint ready to die. Help me die. 22 more day's left help help help

The brawny youth, just five months past his sixteenth birthday, tugged free a nylon drawstring, from the jacket the jailer had allowed him to wear in the cold, dimly lit, windowless cell. Juan knotted one end around a heavy, wire-mesh ventilation grill and the other end about his throat. Then, standing a few inches from the wall, Juan let his knees collapse.

The sheriff rushed into the cell and cut him loose. However, the officer's desperate efforts to revive Juan failed. The boy was dead.

Several days later, the *Des Moines Register and Tribune* quoted the sheriff. "He didn't jump off of anything. He just slumped down. He could have stood up at any time before he passed out. But he didn't. He was determined to die."

The phrase "determined to die" is reminiscent of a custom of another American minority: the Native American. The Plains tribe has a tradition known as "Crazy-Dog-Wishing-To-Die." This is a role assumed by a member of a tribe because he is in mourning or he has been insulted. Once a man has declared himself to be a "Crazy-Dog," he must do everything in reverse. He will say the opposite of what he means, and he must attack the enemy until either they or he are dead.

In 1969, a research team reported that the Sioux, a Plains tribe, had a high death rate from accidents; in fact, accidents were their second greatest cause of death. On the other hand, the Sioux have no recorded suicides, nor are they willing to discuss death with nongroup members. Yet incident after incident occurs where men deliberately walk into the traffic on busy freeways or fight barroom brawls to lose.

Both seem to indicate the "Crazy-Dog" tradition continues; both seem another way to be "determined to die."

The problem of suicide among Native Americans has reached scare-headline proportions. One informational paper will state that the Indian suicide rate is higher than any other subgroup of the American population. Another public affairs leaflet tells us the suicide rate among Indians is ten times the national average.

Suicide *is* a major health problem among Native Americans as it is for all segments of the United States population. Verifying the degree of self-destructive behavior among Indians is difficult. First, though there have been many studies completed about the various Indian groups, few of them contain any investigations into suicide. Most figures available about Indian suicides have been compiled to justify the creation of a suicide-prevention program or to evaluate the success or failure of an already established program. Statistics can be made to play games. If a tribe has one suicide in one year and two suicides the following year, a report can state honestly that the suicide rate for that tribe doubled in one year. The second problem related to investigating the question of suicide among Native Americans is that there is no one overall common suicide pattern linking the various tribes.

The Shoshone Indians are the group that has provided the often quoted suicide rate of 100 per 100,000 population, or ten times the national rate.

This high ratio is prevalent among adolescent males who have histories of school and drug problems. Also characteristic of these suicides' lives were a high level of family disorganization and unemployment problems.

Among the Uto-Aztecan speakers of the Southwestern Desert (Pima, Papago and Yaquis), suicide again appears to be mainly a male problem. Leaders of the tribes view suicide as an indication that there is a serious breakdown of the community.

The values of reservation society conflicting with those of mainstream America may be another cause of Native American suicide. Decisions by tribal councils about what is best for the tribe and its individual members may seem restrictive to a young person who has developed a firm belief in the rights of the individual. On the other hand, with the dissolution of the tribal structure, another member may see no future among his own people. But, off the reservation, he finds the only employment available is a low-paying menial job. Prejudice is high in many communities bordering Indian reservations. There is no way up anywhere. Often the person turns to heavy drinking for consolation. This results in health problems as well as family arguments and the breakdown of marriages.

Family strife figures as an important factor in suicides in the White Mountain Apache tribe and the Navajos. One report determined that forty-three out of fifty-six Apache suicides were precipitated by "bad words" or verbal fighting with a family member or

spouse. The people whom the researcher interviewed indicated that aggression figured importantly
in the suicides. The Apaches have a history of being
more aggressive than most tribes, but today they
cannot kill the person with whom they are angry or
they will be charged with murder. So if someone really wants to hurt another person, he or she may
commit suicide, leaving the hated individual to deal
with the grief and the animosity of the community.

Although the Navajo Indians have a low suicide
rate, there is one telltale characteristic of their suicides. They almost always occur near the place of
residence. Investigators say this is a further indication that the motivation was a family fight. The Navajos believe that anyone finding the body of a suicide is threatened by danger. This is especially true
if the finder is a family member. So the suicide, in
effect, is a way of inflicting punishment upon the
family by committing the deed near the home. The
probability is great that the body will be found by a
family member.

An important factor influencing the overall Native
American suicide problem is public opinion and the
self-image. Indians are constantly portrayed in scientific reports, the news media, and the arts as having a
noble past, a sad present, and no future on or off
the reservation. This constant depiction cannot help
but lower the self-esteem of many young Indians.

A low self-image is also a cause of black suicide.
People mistakenly tend to think of suicide as a white
problem, but the figures for black suicide, especially

in urban areas, are high. For blacks the most danger-ous years are the young years, while for whites the suicide rates jump noticeably after the age of forty-five.

Most unhappy young adult whites feel that things will get better "when I grow up." And often they are right. A feeling of hopelessness usually comes in their mid-forties when they realize that their life is now quite well set. If they have not achieved their dreams, time and age are now against them. For blacks, however, racism has already implanted a feel-ing that the future will never be satisfying. This at-tack on their dreams has frequently occurred even before they enter school. Therefore, many see no value to education, for it appears to have no rele-vance to their everyday lives. If they later change their minds, the new attitude may come too late, for they might not have developed the capacity for sus-tained effort. This point of view is often carried over to their jobs. Having abandoned the hopes they may have had, they do not see employment changing their future.

"There's no place for me to go," said one young, urban black.

If the outside world is unkind, the pressures of family life are even more cruel for city blacks. The absence of a father figure is the single most devastat-ing factor of black family life and can often perpetu-ate problems for several generations. If the man was violent, beating his wife and children before he de-serted them, the effect is even worse.

For black females, the feeling of having been abandoned by their fathers when young cause them to mistrust males. Certain black males, having been deserted by their fathers, which they view as rejection, and afflicted with their mother's subsequent hatred of men, find heterosexuality frightening. Homosexuality seems an escape.

Dwight T. is a young black currently living at a halfway house. Five months ago, at the age of sixteen, he was on the brink of suicide. That, along with his drug problem, motivated him to enter a rehabilitation center. The center is not located in the city where his mother and two sisters live.

"Far away, man. As far as I could get. *She* was it. My trouble."

The "she" is his mother. Dwight, though from ghetto background and a school dropout, is well-spoken without relying on many Black-English expressions. He claims this was because of a teacher who helped him to "speak right." The teacher subsequently found another job and left Dwight's school. Further questions on this subject are answered by shrugged shoulders. Dwight is not ready to explore this loss.

But he does discuss his home freely, though with bitterness. Whenever he refers to his mother, the "she" and "her" are heavily emphasized.

"No, I never knew him [my father]. He split early. And who can blame him? All she can do is bitch. I mean it—all day long. And then she really fucked me. She took in Jimmy."

Jimmy is Dwight's nineteen-year-old cousin. He was told to leave his own home. His mother would not take him back after he had served a prison sentence for robbery. Fifteen-year-old Dwight idolized Jimmy.

"When you were on the street with him, man, you were *safe*. Nobody messed with Jimmy. We could go anywhere. He was it. *The* one." Dwight's home was a small apartment, so Jimmy and Dwight shared a couch for sleeping. Then one night Jimmy made sexual advances. "I couldn't believe it. But if Jimmy was doing that, it must be all right. He was no queer. Soon every night we'd get into it [have sexual relations]. Sometimes when she—my mother—was gone, we'd use her bed. He taught me how—how to do things to him. You know?

"He also got me into drugs. I had stayed clean. And that was hard. But I did it. But Jimmy kept getting stuff, and I was into that." One day Jimmy announced that he was getting married and would move in with a friend within a few days. The wedding would be held in several months. "When I asked him to let me visit, he said, 'Shit, I don't want no fucking queer hanging around me.' I couldn't believe it."

Dwight experienced a tremendous loss when Jimmy left the apartment. Soon after, he was to feel betrayed. His source of drugs was gone. Within a few days, he was approached by a street pusher. The man would provide the drugs but wanted sexual favors in return. "Jimmy told him about me. He must've. Shit, how many others did he tell? I won't tell you—or anyone—what that fat fucker [the dealer] used to make me do.

"One night I couldn't go there any more. Nothing in the world would make me go, *Nothing,* man! I went up [onto] the roof to jump. But there was this dude and his lady. I left and called for help [professional advice]. Because I was going to do it, man. I was going to do it."

Ironically, Dwight used the same phrase later in his interview. The organization Dwight telephoned had helped him to be admitted to the center where he now lives full-time. He insists, "I'm going to do it." Now he means pulling himself and his life together. Enough time has not passed for him to sort out his problems. But his brown eyes gleam with determination, and one feels that Dwight will, indeed, "do it."

The experiences Dwight suffered and his suicide attempt reflect another aspect of black suicide. In New York City, where many blacks spend most of their lives in and on top of tenement buildings, approximately fifty to sixty percent of black suicides each year are by jumping. Leaping from the roofs of these buildings is possibly the closest these blacks get to feeling they can escape ghetto life.

For all minorities, society must bear part of the guilt for the suicide rate. On the one hand we promise that everything is available through education, employment, and hard work. Then once we have stimulated the desires of minority peoples, we savagely destroy any hope of fulfillment by discrimination. The rage and self-hatred induced by society's rejection is a leading factor in the suicide attempts by many members of American minorities.

5

Suicide in Other Countries

As already mentioned, the World Health Organization (WHO) held its 1974 conference in Luxembourg to focus on suicide as a problem among the young. In September 1975, the Eighth International Congress on Suicide Prevention was conducted with approximately 500 psychiatrists from twenty-one nations assembling in Jerusalem. More than 100 papers on the social and psychological aspects of suicide were presented for the members' attention.

What is the significance of these international meetings?

With the increasing public awareness about youthful suicide in the United States, many people are beginning to consider the situation as purely an American problem, but the tragedy of suicide is international in scope. In most cases, however, conditions within the individual country somehow seem to exert an influence over the suicide rate. For example, there are "high" and "low" suicide countries. Spain has a very low rate; Japan, high.

The quest to find reasons and possible common strands among nations has produced a flurry of fallacies about the relationship of suicide to a particular nationality. For instance, there is the myth that countries that are predominantly Catholic in religion have a lower rate than Protestant nations. The reason, some people claim, is that the Catholic church is adamantly against suicide, and therefore the people are less prone to view it as an acceptable action. But when the facts are checked, this theory does not always prove true. France, largely Catholic, has a high suicide rate, while Norway, largely Protestant, has a low rate.

Another often-quoted theory deals with highly civilized countries versus underdeveloped nations in their respective suicide rates. Some people insist that suicide is the price of being a highly developed nation. Again, little actual proof exists to support this idea. First, information regarding suicides is difficult to obtain from many emerging nations and if secured, is often inaccurate. Also, some highly developed nations, such as Holland, have a very low suicide rate.

If the latter theory is ever substantiated, believers state, it will be because of two possible influential factors. One is that in well-developed nations there is a tendency for children to attend school at progressively earlier ages. The less a very young child is around its parents, the more danger exists that the youngster will have a feeling of rejection. The other reason is that frequently in the undeveloped countries, the citizens are devoting all their energies to building for the future. Their goal, to raise their country to the standards of other nations, gives a direction and purpose to life that tends to act as an antidote to suicide.

Further research will have to be done before investigators can decide whether these are valid theories or merely more myths.

Perhaps the most widespread misconception about suicide and a specific nation was started in the United States. President Dwight D. Eisenhower referred in a speech to a "friendly European nation" which, as a result of "almost complete paternalism," had experienced a sharp rise in suicides.

Immediately, some people assumed Sweden was the culprit and placed the blame for that country's high suicide rate on its political system. Those persons who agreed with President Eisenhower and other political conservatives say that a high degree of socialism destroys individual incentive, fosters boredom, and fails to develop tough, resilient people. When a person is unable to face life's difficulties, minor troubles might loom larger than they actually are and could push the person to suicide. Or, as the psychologists say, the adaptation level for frustration is reduced in these people.

Authorities who oppose that view have more solid evidence for their arguments. There is little documentation to prove that welfare states have a higher incidence of suicide than other countries. Norway is a welfare state but has a low suicide rate. Denmark had a high level of suicides long before it became a welfare state. With the introduction of social reforms, Denmark's suicide statistics exhibited a moderate decline. Saskatchewan, which is perhaps the most advanced welfare state in Canada, has a somewhat lower suicide ratio than its neighboring provinces of Alberta and Manitoba.

Psychologically, there is no evidence to show that a nation with many social welfare programs is producing damaged personalities. In fact, the Swedes are characterized by a high degree of incentive, approaching their responsibilities with perhaps even more vigor and determination than Americans. Nor is there any link between boredom and suicide. Suicide is most often a result of rejection, emotional deprivation, and despair. A welfare state produces a hopeful outlook for the future. If anything, this perspective should decrease the suicide rate.

And finally, as Maurice L. Farber wrote in *Theory of Suicide*, "No one ever committed suicide because he or she received a social security check."

If myths abound about the relationship of nationality and suicide, what proven constants were found which affect suicide in various countries? There are several that have received wide, general acceptance.

A single, dramatic event that seems to threaten the individual's happiness or the future of the nation. For example, when President Franklin D. Roosevelt died, there was a sharp rise in suicides in the United States and also in the countries of the Allies. People felt Roosevelt's death might affect the outcome of World War II. Before the Berlin Wall was closed in 1961, the suicide rate in East Berlin was about one a day. A few days after the closing, the rate had climbed to twenty-five a day.

Among young people, a motivating factor for suicide could be the dramatic death of a hero or idol. In April 1977, a very popular singer died in Egypt. Within a few days a number of teenage girls had killed themselves because of his death.

Strong demands for the individual to display competence. This factor, rather than the welfare state theory, may be more directly related to the high degree of suicide in Sweden as it is among youthful Japanese. Further explanation will be provided in this chapter when the high suicide rate of Japanese young people is discussed.

Lack of people or institutions providing emotional support. The role of the family in the daily life of a growing child has a great effect on how that child will combat problems when he or she is older. The Irish and Italians have a strong sense of family, and the suicide rates in their home countries are low. Comparing Denmark (high) to Norway (low), there is a marked difference in the part parents play in their children's lives. There are more working mothers in Denmark than Norway, and consequently many infant day nurseries operate in Denmark while Norway has few. Norwegian mothers devote much time to caring for their babies, and

Norwegian fathers are important in the nuclear family. Norwegian men generally spend time training and encouraging their children.

Cultural attitude toward suicide. Though suicide in some cases may be an attempt to inflict punishment on the survivors, statistics seem to indicate that where the people of a nation are strongly against suicide, the rate is low (Norway). The Danes are more tolerant of suicide, and their national rate is high.

Recently, there has been a rapid growth of "Right-to-Die" movements around the world. These organizations are most successful in those countries that already have a high degree of suicide. In the United States, California, a state with one of the highest suicide rates, has voted a state law permitting a patient with a terminal illness to be allowed to die if he or she does not want life prolonged through mechanical means.

In European countries, Right-to-Die groups have been most effective in Britain, Sweden, and Denmark, which have high suicide rates. This appears to indicate a cultural acceptance of suicide. But, even in these countries, debates rage about a person's right to choose life or death.

In November, 1975, Dr. Miriam Stoppard, thirty-seven-year-old wife of the English playwright Tom Stoppard, admitted on a television program that she had once unplugged life-supporting equipment to allow a brain-damaged patient to die. According to

Dr. Stoppard, this was something doctors do "every day of the week."

Dr. Uri Lowental, an Israeli psychiatrist, was quoted in the October 26, 1975, *New York Times* as saying that suicide is sometimes a realistic solution to an individual's dilemma. He cited case histories where this move might be a correct one, such as "a cancer patient who terminates his suffering, a schizophrenic who exchanges lifelong mental hollowness with eternal serenity, or occasionally, an aged person who masters the quality and quantity of his approaching, inevitable death."

But there are those opposed to this philosophy, and they have telling facts at their disposal. The *London Daily Telegraph* in October, 1975, described the case history of twenty-six-year-old Steven Talbot. Steve had been in a motorcycle accident and was diagnosed by physicians as a hopeless case. Rather than opting to end his life, Steve struggled to overcome the effects of his injuries. Today, Steve Talbot uses a wheelchair for movement and has a responsible job handling bookings for a London hotel.

The *Daily Telegraph* editorialized: "The case of Steve Talbot is a powerful reminder of why society must think deeply and carefully before delegating to anyone the right to end life."

These four elements—cultural attitude, lack of emotional support, demands to succeed, frightening event—may well explain why Japan has one of the leading suicide rates in the world.

The uniqueness about Japan in contrast to Western countries is that, in the West, suicide rates generally increase with age. Japan, however, shows two peaks for suicides: the young and the aged. Also, the Japanese suicide rate for females is the highest among modern nations. The rate for Japanese female suicides in 1963 was six times that for America. The United States did experience a growth in female suicides during the sixties, so by 1967 Japan's rate was only 1.6 times as great as this country's.

There is another notable contrast between Japanese suicides and those in the Western nations. In most Western countries suicide appears to be more an urban problem than a rural one, although suicides do occur in both areas. The suicide statistics of Japan reflect no noticeable difference between city and country regions.

Why should Japan be among the leaders in the problem of youthful suicides? Consider the nation in terms of the four constants already mentioned.

Cultural Attitude: For over 1,000 years in Japan, suicide or hara-kiri has been considered the honorable action to escape surrender to an enemy or to avoid disgrace. Though hara-kiri was outlawed in 1868, death with honor is still a strong ingredient of Japanese life.

On November 25, 1970, Yukio Mishima, a candidate for the Nobel Prize for literature, committed suicide with one of his followers. His purpose was to convince his countrymen to return to the old ways, one of which was an "honorable death." More recently, in 1975, an executive of a Japanese catering firm which provided the food served on Japan Air Lines killed himself. The reason was that his company's food had poisoned 143 passengers on a flight. Though he himself was in no way responsible for the tainted food, the disgrace fell upon him as the head of the company.

Another basic belief of many Japanese people is the Buddhist concept of *mujo-kan*. This philosophy sees the human body as the temporary home for the soul. Thus, biological living is not the supreme height that man can reach and may well be without meaning.

Combining these two cultural threads—the image of dying honorably and the view of life on earth as meaningless—there is a definite psychological preparation for Japanese people to view suicide as a viable solution to their problems.

Cultural values also affect the second factor.

Lack of Emotional Support: One of the most stated reasons for youthful Japanese suicides is the conflict between the young and the old; the modern and the traditional. This statement is a bit misleading. First, cultural conflict disturbs those aged persons who commit suicide, too. Cultural change by itself, however, cannot produce suicide. If that were true, Tokyo, the Japanese city which has been transformed the most extensively since the end of World War II, would have the highest suicide rate. Tokyo, in fact, has a lower rate than certain other areas. The reason for this is because Tokyo's change has been so complete.

The deciding factor linking suicide and social change seems to be the scissor effect, which occurs if one portion of the population determinedly retains the traditional values while another group is working equally hard to bring about acceptance of different attitudes. This ripping force influences both the aged and the young in Japan: the double peaks for Japanese suicides.

When people deny our beliefs, we often believe they are denying us. Older Japanese persons who cannot adapt to social change and feel shunted to the sidelines will frequently commit suicide. The youngsters find a growing rift between their parents and grandparents on one side and their peer group and its values on the other. The older people negate the new culture and, in effect, reject the youngsters at the same time. The children then grow up in an environment that breeds insecurity.

Demands to Succeed and *Dramatic, Frightening Event:* The youngsters mature, absorbing an attitude which is oddly typical of both their traditional culture and the new Western influences: the demand to succeed.

Success is very important to the Japanese people, but the value of the success is measured solely by how much their fellow countrymen admire their good fortune. In Japan, as in few other nations, there is a precise moment that designates success or failure: the admission into a good university. Without this higher education, there is little hope for success, so the days of the testing and the arrival of the final results are desperate ones for Japanese young people. Failure is traumatic and one of the most frequent reasons for suicide among Japanese youths.

Reviewing the causes of suicide in countries around the world, we can see there is little difference between foreign countries and the United States. Family life, especially for the very young, is a major factor in producing a sense of competence within a child, whether it be Buffalo, New York, or Bergen, Norway. A single frightening moment, which threatens future happiness, can prompt a young person to suicide in Kyoto, Japan, or Kansas City, Missouri. The seeds of suicide are, indeed, planted in our culture, and cultures around the world display certain similarities. Perhaps more answers to the question of suicide will come through combined, international efforts.

6

Suicidal Equivalents

As amazing as it may sound, there are people all around us who are actively and methodically trying to kill themselves without ever realizing it. In a way, the unconscious mind of this type of person keeps feeding the conscious mind excuses which blot out the reality of his or her actions. Some people do recognize their self-destructiveness; others deny it till the day they die.

The phrase "death wish" is often bandied about by people who have acquired a few isolated facts and wish to display their dime-store education in psychology.

"You're smoking three packs a day? You must have a death wish," says one person.

Another individual remarks, "People who drive too fast have a death wish."

"You drink because you want to destroy yourself," a third person may say pontifically.

Though their information is often scanty and misleading, these people are frequently surprisingly right. Sigmund Freud, the pioneer in the study of the unconscious mind, said that everyone has a desire to harm or even totally destroy him- or herself. Some people, because of the unfortunate circumstances of their lives, are driven to suicide openly and consciously. Others seek more subtle, slower means without comprehending why or what they are doing. Certain persons are able to perceive the consequences of their self-destructive urges and change their direction. As a rule, most people are able to control these negative impulses fairly well and live normal, happy lives.

Even some animals display this desire to inflict injury upon themselves or surrender to death. Scientists have noted that monkeys who were deprived of their mothers and were forced to grow up alone often engage in self-biting.

Hope is not a purely human emotion though only humans have recognized and labelled the feeling. Animals may exhibit a very primitive type of hope. Eliminate that hope and, like human beings, they lose the will to live. A domestic cat, mortally ill, will often "crawl away to die." And there are birds who rest beside the body of their dead mate until they too die.

If that cat or bird were a human being, we might place the animal under the category of *Those Who Surrender to Death*. The human mind is a fantastic mechanism. Determination and drive can accomplish great feats. There are recorded case histories of cancer that has been diagnosed as terminal by several physicians that suddenly underwent a reversal, and soon the patient had fully recovered. The miraculous cure? The person's fierce desire to survive?

Consider also the workings of voodoo, frequently portrayed on television and in motion pictures as an eerie and often unbelievable practice. Yet, thousands of people fear voodooism because they have seen its success. The procedure usually follows these lines. A person goes to a witchdoctor and pays him to destroy an enemy. The witch doctor leaves a talisman on the doorstep where the second person is certain to find the object. Shortly after the discovery of the feared token, the victim begins to waste away. Despite medical attention, the person eventually dies.

Witchcraft? Magic spells? Neither, most likely. Research has shown that voodooism only works on those who truly believe in its powers. Therefore, once the individual knows a spell has been cast, his or her own mind does the evil work.

The above-mentioned victim is an example of *Those Who Surrender to Death*. These are people who either scare themselves to death or give into death, such as the person who has experienced a severe disappointment or emotional shock. He or she will sit back and get ready to die without realizing or acknowledging that fact. The person does not eat and cannot sleep. If warned about possible illness, he or she will reply, "I'll eat something later."

Generally, the severity of the unhappiness wears

off in time, and the human instinct for survival regains control. Slowly, steadily, the person begins to resume a normal life. For others, however, "later" never comes. The submerged desire for death is too strong. These people lose weight, becoming increasingly weaker until death finally claims them.

A second group of people who suffer from a suicidal equivalent could be labelled *Those Who Mock Death*. These are persons who engage in activities which seem to play games with death, who dare death to take them if it can. Their unconscious minds pump various excuses into their conscious thoughts.

"I'm brave if I do this."

"I'm better than everybody else because they're too scared to try it."

"I don't have a death wish. I've just got a wicked competitive spirit."

The last is an actual quote from George C. During the day, twenty-three-year-old George C. is a seventh grade mathematics teacher. On summer weekends, he is an auto racing driver. George spent several thousand dollars to build his own race car which, owing to the nature of the sport, cannot be insured. Neither can George. He admits that he's a "great street driver but only an okay racer." Yet he never misses a race even if the winning prize is only twenty-five or fifty dollars. George has only won three races in his life; one for a prize of three cans of motor oil.

On a July night in 1976, while rounding the second turn of a Massachusetts race track, George's vehicle was bumped by another car, spun out of control, and slammed into a concrete wall. The car flipped over. The crowd gasped and then rushed eagerly to the railing to see what they could.

Thanks to safety belts and roll bars, George was not badly injured. An overnight stay in the hospital and a few weeks around the house nursing his painful, taped ribs, were his only physical reminders of the accident. Despite pleadings by his wife to consider their one-year-old daughter, George was already planning to borrow money to repair the heavily damaged car and continue racing.

"My friends keep telling me I've got a death wish," he recently told an interviewer. "But they're wrong. I don't have a death wish. I've just got a wicked competitive spirit."

Two thousand miles away and eight months later, Joe E. of Houston, Texas, was with his friends on an evening in March 1977. The eighteen-year-old boy removed a gun from his dresser and dared his companions to play Russian Roulette. Placing the barrel against his temple, he asked, "Who wants to play? I'll go first." He pulled the trigger.

Both George C. and Joe E. may well be included as members of *Those Who Mock Death*. Only one of them is still alive; the other died of a head wound.

Another category of suicidal equivalents could be titled *Those Who Hasten Death*. In this class would be those people who are in danger of ruining their health or bringing about their deaths by overindulgence in tobacco, alcohol, drugs, food, and reckless driving. This is the most recognizable group and, perhaps for that reason, seems more prevalent than others. Also, peculiar to this category, is the fact that more members do admit to themselves that their behavior is self-destructive. Yet they still can find overriding reasons to continue along their downhill paths.

Certainly, any individual who is a heavy smoker must be aware of the health dangers. There has been enormous research, thoroughly publicized, into the effects of the cancer-producing agents in cigarettes, so that it is no longer speculative that there is a link between that disease and smoking.

Alcoholism is now rampant among young people, although it has not yet created the massive public outburst which the rise in drug use did during the 1960s. One reason is that drinking still has broad social acceptance. In fact, there are fathers who even now smile nostalgically when their teenage son comes home drunk for the first time.

Recently, parents in a Long Island community did not smile, however, when they learned their eleven-year-old sons and daughters were bringing Scotch to school in small milk containers and drinking the liquor during lunch. The adults supervising the cafeteria only saw sixth grade children sipping on their milk straws; the afternoon teachers saw these youngsters heavily intoxicated.

Perhaps the overindulgence least recognized as a suicidal equivalent is overeating. Though our current concept of beauty is "thin is in," many people still find fatness amusing—especially if they are not fat themselves. Phrases like "fat and jolly" dot our everyday language, while overweight comedians wobble before us on our television screens, eliciting laughs with jokes about their own obesity. Drug addiction and acute alcoholism are the subjects for serious television documentaries, but obesity is usually reserved for the comedy hours.

Though dealing in stereotypes is risky, corpulent people seem to come in two major varieties. There are the complainers, the whiners, the ones who go through life glowering at the world around them. These people are the first to attack any physical defect or poor habit in another person. Possibly, they are employing a defensive strategy. The others are the ones who seem happy and cheery at all times. But if one checks closely, that sudden laugh may be a shield and the flashing smile a sword to ward off injurious remarks or at best hide wounds. Judi T. is one of the latter.

"Yeah, my friends make jokes because I'm fat. But they don't mean nothing. Kind of nice in a way. You know what I mean?"

Judi is nineteen years old, works as a secretary during the day, and at night sings in an amateur choral group in a Midwestern city.

"It [the weight] is good for my voice," she explains.

The weight that is good for her voice registers "around 270 pounds," which is quite a bit to carry for a person who is only five feet, three inches tall. When asked if she realizes that the weight, which produces rich notes, can be dangerous and is directly related to diabetes and especially heart attacks in fat people fifty to sixty years old, her sudden, full-bodied laugh erupts again as does the gleaming smile.

"Fifty or sixty? That's years from now."

Growing up as an only child, she considered her parents nice people. Her father still works as a post-man, and her mother is the "typical housewife." Judi admits that her parents didn't really understand her problems, but they tried to be extra kind to her when they saw that she was hurting physically or emotionally. Her mother would prepare a special dinner on those "gunky days" and would announce to her husband that "tonight this is Judi's dinner" and "Judi's apple pie." The remedy almost always worked a cure.

Does it still act as a cure?

"Yeah, whenever I'm mad or upset, I do eat more." But Judi could not see the similarity of that practice to the person who smokes or drinks when emotional stress is present.

Judi has traveled the route that many overweight people follow. The clubs that promised to encourage their members to take off weight annoyed her be-cause they were always filled with loud-voiced old women who "swore like sailors." Then she tried the doctor routine. She disliked the green pills that made her feel high and the "water pills" that resulted in embarrassing emergencies. Besides, the weight went down and the weight went up. Same pattern. Down and up. Telling people her condition was glandular was easier than running off to doctors all the time and cheaper than paying their bills.

Obese people who have duplicated Judi's efforts might well have saved the money from all those medical bills and funnelled the cash into psychotherapy. For many, their overeating is not merely a poor nutritional habit, but an addiction as serious as smoking, drug use, or drinking.

Another sort of individual who may rank as one of *Those Who Hasten Death* is the reckless driver. As mentioned earlier, the number one killer of young people in the United States today is automobile accidents. Some of these may be deliberate suicides; others, suicide equivalents. To claim that young people are too inexperienced to be good drivers would be an oversimplification. Most experts agree that it is not how a person learned to drive a car, which affects the way he or she will drive, but the driver's personality.

In an article entitled, "Teenagers: How they feel is how they drive" in the March 2, 1975, *New York Times,* Gerald Astor surveyed sociologists and psychologists on the subject of young drivers. He found that his interviewees "blame cultural factors for the high rate of accidents among young people." These would include concern about college or employment, poor school grades, and the fear of assuming the responsibilities of an adult. The same article quoted

Dr. David Klein, social science professor at Michigan State University. He believes that the young driver "may quite deliberately engage in deviate behavior that expresses his (or her) resentment or defiance."

Hostility and aggression and the fear of coping are also related to many known suicides.

A final classification among the major suicide equivalents attracted public attention in November, 1976, when Gary Mark Gilmore brought legal action against the State of Utah, demanding they carry out his death penalty for murder. This group could be named *Those Who Seek Death by the Hands of Others*. Numerous psychiatric case histories reveal people, living tormented lives, who murder others with the conscious or unconscious intention of receiving the death penalty. Whether they realize they lack the nerve to kill themselves or whether they merely seek an end to their unhappiness, they frequently have conscious thoughts that their crime will definitely result in their deaths.

Sean M. grew up on the fringe of the Bedford-Stuyvesant section of Brooklyn in the late 1950s and early 1960s. His Irish parents instilled a deep prejudice in him against blacks, which was reenforced by his racially mixed neighborhood. A shy child, Sean's early years and midteens were filled with dreams of love and fantasies of power. Emotional injuries could only be alleviated by aggressive acts against other people, using knives and zip guns he had built himself.

Floating through each day, Sean felt as though life

was a movie. He thought he knew the script and frequently heard the background music. One night, after a serious argument with his girl friend, sixteen-year-old Sean took the shotgun he kept hidden in the basement and went to a nearby street corner. The first person he saw was a black man about thirty years old.

"I never seen him before—and I wouldn't say I didn't know what killing meant. I really didn't know that when you were going to kill someone that you're taking their life. I didn't understand that. But the reason was that I wanted to kill myself. That was the whole reason behind that—because of that girl, I really wanted to kill myself. But I just couldn't do it. I just could not take my own life. I just didn't have the courage to do that. Watching movies and all, I thought this would be a nice way to go. The electric chair would be terrific. Because of glorification. If you watch movies, you see how glorified it is. And that impressed me."

Sean aimed the gun, pulled the trigger, and prayed all his misery would end. He was arrested two days later for murder. Two police officers questioned him at the local precinct.

"They played all their usual tricks, but they weren't fooling me. I had seen them all in movies. But what really happened was I wanted to get caught. So I confessed to it, and that was the beginning of prison."

The end of prison came fourteen years later when Sean was released on parole. Today, he has exorcised his demons and is living a productive life no longer threatened by self-destructive impulses.

If anyone recognizes such tendencies within her- or himself, there is professional help available, often at no charge. Though suffering from one of the suicidal equivalents may not seem as dangerous as being suicidal, the condition can be even more insidious. The person may not realize where the road is leading and, therefore, never see a need to cry for help.

7

Suicide Prevention— Internal

"Late one afternoon, I went to visit my friend—or more appropriately, my acquaintance. She always left her door open, so I went inside, and sat down at the desk. She would never know I was there. In fact, she seemed disturbingly unaware of my presence in general. So I went through her things. I found mostly old school papers with low grades on them. Then, I found her architectural design knife. It had a retractable blade that was very much like a razor blade.

"Suddenly, I got a passionate urge to obliterate myself. In most ways, I felt obliterated already, so why not finish the job? It would be the realistic and gutsy thing to do under the circumstances. So I started cutting my wrists."

Fortunately for Danise E., she did not succeed in

this suicide attempt. She found she had too many small veins and the blood kept clotting. When the first frenzied moments of the attempt passed, she became less violent about her goal.

"I decided that I was a coward and that I would just have to go on living. I didn't think anything would improve, though. I just felt that I was doomed to live through a lot more pain, and there was nothing I could do about it.

"I cleaned the knife with Kleenex and managed to restore the room to its original condition. My friend never noticed anything amiss."

Danise did live through a few more months of pain before her problems with poor college grades, an unhappy affair with her boyfriend, and an unpleasant home situation began to clear up. But matters did clear up. That's the important thing.

And so will your problems.

Conceivably, some readers of this book may be contemplating suicide. If so, you are probably frantically searching for answers and help from any source. Suicidal persons are plagued with ambivalent feelings. You want to die, but you want to live. The thought keeps jumping at you. "If only there was some way I could keep on living." Then, this wish is fought down with opposing images of all the troubles piled on your head. Slowly, chillingly, you know the truth. You *must* kill yourself.

But you're wrong.

Right now you won't accept this from me. But no one must commit suicide. There is always an answer to be found. And that is the thing you *must* do. Search for that answer. Obviously, no one answer will fit everyone's needs. Somewhere in this chapter you may find one small thing to show you that there is a need for you in this world.

The severe mental depression which often precedes suicide has several terrible effects. One of the most common is a lowered self-image. You can find nothing good about yourself or your life. Physically and emotionally, you see yourself as an un-nice person. In all probability just the reverse is true about the real you. People who have been hurt by life are usually the nice people in this world. They are generally more sensitive to the needs of others and are less likely ever to treat others as cruelly as they themselves have been treated.

So, perhaps the first thing you might do—rather than face all your problems yet—is take an honest look at yourself. A young man of seventeen, Shawn F., who was interviewed for this book, did that as a last, desperate action. The revolver was loaded and on the table before him. On sheer impulse, he decided to list all the positives in his life. In a way, he confided to the interviewer, he wanted to see how much the world was losing by his death. Later, he planned to tear the list to shreds and pull the trigger.

Writing down all your good qualities may sound foolish, because they are in your head already. But, mentally, they are mixed in with all the negatives, which often overshadow them or blot them out.

Shawn admitted that in the first few minutes he

only found two good things and had to resist writing all the wrong things. There seemed to be so many wrong things. So he made another column and began listing the names of all the people who would sincerely miss him when he was dead. This he found easier to do and at the same time discovered some more good qualities to add to the first section.

Fifteen minutes later, he stared at the paper in amazement. The lists were longer than he had expected. For a little while, he kept rereading what he had written, thinking. He did not tear the paper to shreds. In fact, he still has the sheet today, three years later. He keeps it as a reminder of how close he had come to doing "the dumbest thing I could have done."

Making such a list, of course, does nothing to eliminate the problems facing you. But it may get you past the "suicidal crisis," those minutes when you are in the process of killing yourself. You have made the decision and are preparing the means. Be aware that the suicidal crisis is of short duration. One psychiatrist said that the period usually lasts no longer than ten minutes.

Ten minutes separate you from death. If you can just get through them, you'll be able to start putting your life together. In preparing this book, I spoke with thirteen people who had attempted suicide. All of them regretted the attempt and realize now that suicide definitely would not have been the solution.

What else can you do to get past this suicidal crisis period?

Talk to someone!

There is nothing worse than being by yourself when you are suffering from some emotional stress. Being a writer is a lonely business with many disappointments. At times I get to feeling down. I'm lucky enough to have a friend whom I can call, just to say I feel like talking to someone, and we discuss everyday matters. A short while later, the bad mood is gone, and I'm working at my typewriter again. And I was merely experiencing a mild depression.

For Gladys V., a family member was there to help her through the suicidal crisis. "My mother was my best friend at the time. My mother was a very good mother, very warm and loving. Yeah, my mother was always there."

A good friend helped Steve H. to keep living. "I had one very close friend. When I first went to college, I met him in my first year, and we were very tight. It got to the point where we were so tight that we could finish each other's sentences. He'd listen when I talked about being depressed and being upset. We'd talk about that at great length."

If you don't feel you can talk to a family member or a friend, then you might talk to a member of the clergy or to your family doctor. If there seems to be no one in your life whom you feel you can trust and speak with honestly, then call a nearby crisis center. Don't think that a stranger would not be interested in your problems. I have met some volunteers who work for a suicide prevention center, and I would not hesitate to call them. These people are concerned and want to help. They derive great satisfaction from aiding others. One volunteer told me that by helping others through difficulties she felt as though she was leading a fuller, richer life. Also, the fact that the volunteer at a center is not emotionally involved in your problem may make it easier for him or her to guide you to a better understanding of exactly what you can start to do to get your life running straight again. You, too, may find it easier to discuss everything with that person, where you might be reluctant to reveal certain problems to friends or family members. Any information you divulge to a center volunteer is completely confidential. No one will ever learn what you talked about unless you yourself tell.

The crisis center is available as often as you wish. If you find yourself relating well with one particular volunteer, you may leave a message for him or her to call you the next time that person is on duty. The center can give you the name of a referral service if that is what you want. These clinics are usually free. You will generally have an individual consultation there once a week for a period of several months or until things start getting better for you.

Crisis intervention centers are usually listed in the telephone book, but if you cannot find one, ask the operator. There is even a hot-line that you can dial toll-free from anywhere in the United States. The center is called Peace of Mind Hotline, and the headquarters are located in Texas. You can phone them free by dialing: 800-231-6949.

When you call any center, the volunteer answers

by giving the name of the center and says something like, "This is Carolyn. May I help you?"

Listen to the voice, and you will realize the person wants to assist you. You'll probably find yourself feeling a bit better already.

During this same period when things look so hopeless, there is something else that you should do. Get out and do things. When we're upset, we tend to isolate ourselves from others and feel too depressed to take part in the activities we may have participated in before. Yet this is probably the worst thing that we can do. Remaining alone so much causes us to brood continually about our problems. Our minds begin feeding us even darker thoughts. The more unhappy we become, the less clearly we think. Soon even minor difficulties appear insurmountable.

Just being with people who like us or doing something simple like taking a walk through a park on a nice day or playing a fast-paced handball game gives us a badly needed breather from our nonstop worrying. These activities won't make the problems go away, of course. But when we return to a consideration of what is causing us so much anguish, we can think more rationally and take steps to clear away the obstacles blocking us from contentment.

When you are more calm, you have arrived at the time to analyze your problems carefully. There is a problem-solving technique taught in many colleges. The system is simple, yet administrators and executives with complicated duties constantly employ the method.

First, a sizable problem is not going to be solved by

one decisive action. For that matter, perhaps that's why you view your life with despair. There simply does not seem to be the one answer, the single deed that you can perform to eradicate the misery. Before we can unravel an issue, however, we have to break down the question at hand into its component parts. When you are armed with a list of all the small facets, you can then work out solutions for each of these fractional bits.

For example, say you are concerned about your school grades. There will not be *one* thing that you will be able to do that will instantly clear up those poor marks. Separate the problem into smaller parts. Now you realize that actually you are having difficulty with English, biology, and American history. Take each of those individually and continue the refining process. Check American history and you'll see that can be subdivided into smaller points of its own. Possibly in two weeks you are having a test on the economic and social causes of the Civil War. Now you have something you can grab hold of and on which you can work. Clearly, doing well on one test will not mean instant triumph over the big problem, but if you succeed in that small segment and then others, you will eventually affect the total situation.

Undoubtedly, every problem will not separate into small pieces as readily as school work, but all troublesome questions *can* be subdivided into parts A, B, and so forth. If you solve A and B and C, then you will have worked out the massive trouble that seemed to lack any solution.

Don't discard this problem-solving technique without at least attempting to apply the method to your life. The system is viable, and a definite means to fight what may appear to be overwhelmingly dire circumstances.

There is an added benefit to this plan. As you see yourself beginning to solve the component parts, you will feel that you are actively doing something, rather than being continually knocked around by the forces in your life. This encouragement will ignite new ideas and answers that may have eluded you previously. There will be a cumulative effect, and you will soon be on the way to bypassing what seemed mountain-high.

The most important thing to remember is not to lose sight of yourself. When everything is going wrong, we begin to see ourselves as things rather than functional human beings. Each human being has self-dignity and is precious. Whether the person be rich or poor, talented with mind or hands, that life is irreplaceable. You, too, are special.

Even if you don't employ Shawn F.'s scheme of listing your good qualities on a piece of paper, seek them out. Every suicide means the world has lost that rarest of things—life. If you continue to survive, you will be able to bring happiness to those who love you and in some small way make this earth a better place.

Death is the costliest bill possible for the human race.

8

Suicide Prevention—
External

In almost every case, a person contemplating suicide desperately wants help. In fact, the suicide attempt itself is often referred to as a "cry for help" in this book and in professional psychological journals. Frequently, that aid must come from an outside source because the suicidal individual has already considered all the avenues and only complete unhappiness seems to lie ahead. Emotions have colored the situation so heavily that the person is not thinking clearly, but he or she does not understand that. The times we are the most upset, ironically, are the times we think we're acting most rationally. It's only later when we've regained our control that we see how off-base we were in our thinking.

As discussed in the previous chapter, there are private and public agencies involved in suicide prevention; all seek to assist and all do sincere work. Additional information on such agencies will be presented in this and the next chapter. But the single most effective means of preventing the suicide of a close friend or a relative is you. Suicide prevention boils down to a one-to-one relationship. Even the approximately 200 suicide prevention centers across the United States ultimately rely on a single volunteer speaking on the phone to accomplish their goals. Nobody can be more successful in suicide prevention than you if you have educated yourself to the danger signals, the myths, and the best ways to rescue a friend. And a friend is what a suicidal person needs and wants the most. Not a friend who will agree with him or feel sorry for her, but a friend who knows the wisest course of action at a time when the would-be suicide is so distraught that everything appears to be hopeless.

Hopelessness is one of the danger signals of possible suicide. Dr. Jan Fawcett listed five such danger signals in *Before It's Too Late,* a pamphlet published by the American Association of Suicidology. The warning signs are : (1) Mental depression (2) Changes in personality or behavior (3) The making of final arrangements (4) A suicide threat or other statement indicating a desire to die (5) A previous suicide attempt.

Let's examine each of these separately.

1. *Mental Depression:* "Depression is frequently a prelude to suicide," wrote Maurice L. Farber in *Theory of Suicide.* Unfortunately, mental depression is

hard to recognize externally. We all have our public faces and our private faces. A person suffering depression may cloak that feeling while in public, but when alone, the depression sweeps over him or her, drowning the person in despondency.

Perhaps a friend confides that he or she is experiencing sleep disturbances. This may be a clue to depression. Possibly he is awakening much earlier than before or else she has difficulty getting to sleep at night. Excessive sleep may also be a symptom of mental depression. The person may not wish to face life and may prefer to blot out the unhappy hours with sleep. He or she may eventually decide that the eternal sleep of death is the only truly tranquil state.

Other symptoms of mental depression may include loss of appetite, headaches, and general aches and pains as well as psychological symptoms such as anxiety, nervousness, lethargy, crying, and an inability to concentrate.

A danger signal related to mental depression is the paradoxical behavior of a depressed person after he or she decides to commit suicide. The person may seem to be recovering. There are sparks of interest again, and the individual appears to have found the answer to all those heavy burdens. That's the difficulty. The answer may be suicide.

A depressed person sees no avenue to happiness. If he or she settles upon suicide as a solution, suddenly there is an escape. As tragic as it is, this person may actually be enjoying his or her last days, making the final plans, and looking forward to the end of all the troubles. So if you've been helping a young friend or relative through a rough period and suddenly success seems at hand, don't relax your guard. He or she may have entered the most dangerous stage of all.

2. *Changes in Personality or Behavior:* In addition to the symptoms already mentioned under mental depression, there are other personality hints to a potential suicide. There may be a tendency for a person to become uncommunicative and to isolate him- or herself. There is a loss of interest in friends and activities and decreased sexual desire.

Another telltale change might be a discontinuance of a traditional activity. For example, possibly Dave D. goes camping with his friends every Memorial Day weekend. Suddenly, inexplicably, this year he does not want to accompany the others on the backpacking trip. Coupled with other danger signals, this may be a clue to emotional problems leading to suicide.

3. *The Making of Final Arrangements:* The younger the person, the more obvious are these clues. For example, if someone in his or her thirties hires a lawyer to draw up a will, this is normal behavior. There is nothing in this action alone to indicate that he or she is pondering suicide. However, should a fifteen-year-old girl give all her favorite phonograph records to her best friend, saying, "I won't need these any more," that could be a definite clue to possible suicide.

If, as happened recently in Eugene, Oregon, a seventeen-year-old boy gathered his friends one night for a beer party and then acted uncharacteristically, an alert person might have suspected what would happen.

Harry F., usually a quiet, reserved though pleasant person, bid good night to each boy, telling him how much his friendship had meant to him. The boys thought this action strange but attributed the new, demonstrative side of Harry to possibly too much beer. The next morning they learned that Harry had hung himself in the basement room where the party had been held.

4. *A Statement Indicating a Desire to Die or a Suicide Threat:* We all use verbal expressions which might be open to several interpretations. As vacation time nears, someone might say, "It will be so good to get away from it all." A college student, putting in long hours of study before an exam, might exclaim, "Wow! One of these nights I'm going to sleep forever." As a rule these phrases are merely an overexaggeration of our weariness.

A majority of suicidal people make statements such as those above. Unconsciously and, more often, consciously, they are attempts to make those around them aware of the pending attempt. This is why close friends or relatives could be the first to spot the suicidal danger signals. Only people close to another person can detect the tonal difference between someone merely saying they're looking forward to a vacation and a person indicating that life holds too many difficulties for him or her to go on living much longer.

And certainly, a direct threat to commit suicide should *never* be ignored. There is the mistaken belief that those people who vow to kill themselves never really try to end their lives. This myth is absolutely false. Research has shown that four out of five suicides signal their intentions beforehand. Admittedly, some people do this idly to shock friends or in some way to force others to provide love. But these individuals are easily recognized after a few empty threats.

So if someone close to you threatens suicide, follow the cardinal rule of suicide prevention: *Do something.* There are various means to help someone. Suggest a family physician, a clergyman, or a professional counseling service. The most effective person, if you have an emotional bond with the suicidal person, is you. Stay with him or her. The worst thing for such a person is to be alone. Fears can descend upon a solitary person and ravage his or her mind quickly.

If you feel the situation is too difficult for you to handle alone, don't hesitate to contact an older person. Your friend may swear you to secrecy, but what is more important—maintaining a secret or saving your friend's life?

Don't be afraid to discuss suicide with the person. You can't put the thought into his or her head because the possibility has probably been there for some time. Ask questions, give your own sincere feelings, but avoid giving advice. Suggest that sound advice can come from a professional person and make the potential suicide aware of the many services open to him or her.

5. *A Previous Suicide Attempt:* This can be a misleading danger signal. Research shows that only one suicide try in ten is successful, and the overwhelming majority never try again. During the first few months following an attempt, the victim needs moral support and encouragement but does not need people casting suspicious glances in his or her direction. Nor does the individual who attempted suicide need someone around who will overreact to every statement. That can be more damaging than preventive.

But there are those who do attempt again. A teenage girl in Baton Rouge, Louisiana, made three unsuccessful attempts during her high school years. One young man on Long Island, New York, tried five times between the ages of sixteen and twenty-three.

Therefore, if a person has a suicide attempt in his or her past and begins exhibiting some of the danger signals, this may be cause for concern. Don't feel, however, that every former would-be suicide will try again. As we have seen, that's one of the fallacies about suicide.

Fallacies and myths seem intrinsic to suicide and often do great damage. To arm yourself properly to help someone, know the misconceptions about suicide so you can avoid becoming either too little or

too greatly worried. Here are a few of the more popular and most inaccurate fallacies about suicide.

Misconception: "Suicide is a crazy or insane
act."
Fact: Psychologists view suicide as a defensive
action; a problem-solving technique to preserve the integrity of the psychological system
despite its devastating effect on the physical
being.

Misconception: "Suicide is inherited."
Fact: Though historically there appear to be
such examples, research shows that members
of a certain family may develop a belief that
they are "destined" to commit suicide, and
therefore the result is facilitated.

Misconception: "Suicide is the rich man's
curse."
Fact: As shown in an earlier chapter, people
of all different economic, social, and intellec-
tual levels can become suicide statistics. This
misconception may have arisen because a
wealthy person's suicide often seems more
newsworthy than the death of a boy or girl
from the ghetto.

Misconception: "Suicides always occur in bad
weather, spring, or at night."
Fact: There are people who react negatively
to dark, gloomy days, and research shows
that low pressure systems might affect our

emotions. However, the suicide figures do not bear out this statement. Spring, which to many brings the hope of blossoming new life and even love, might contribute to a suicidal person's decision, but again there is little accurate authentication to back up this belief. Most suicides in America occur during the day, as opposed to Japan where they happen at night. However, suicide prevention centers do note that they receive more calls in the evening. This may be due to the fact that many of the callers are simply lonely. During the day they had a degree of companionship at work perhaps, but when the business day was over, they came home to empty rooms. Isolation invites mental depression.

In addition to the one-to-one help a suicidal person should receive, there are other external means which might be utilized to prevent suicide.

First, local, state, and federal governments might make it more difficult to obtain the means that suicidal persons employ. There have been encouraging reports from Washington that the sale of barbiturates might be banned totally. In California, barbiturates are the number one method by which people kill themselves, although guns are number one nationally. More preventive barriers could be constructed on high buildings and bridges. A successful suicide who leaped from the Golden Gate Bridge in San Francisco left a note: "Why did you make it so easy?"

One reason more is not being done along this line is that many people still believe the fallacy that if a person is going to commit suicide, he or she will find a means no matter what people do to prevent the death. They are overlooking the fact that certain suicidal persons are attracted to specific sites. For many years, jumping from the observation deck atop the Empire State Building in New York City seemed the solution to many unhappy people's problems. Once an effective railing was installed, some persons did select other means by which to kill themselves. But others probably reconsidered their problems and sought help rather than death.

Another way to help prevent youthful suicides is a more direct educational attack on both the causes and the means to prevent suicide. In preparation for this book, every state department of education in the United States was contacted and requested to send its guidelines for the state's mental health curriculum.

Of those received, not one provided specific instruction in the dangers of youthful suicide or in suicide prevention. All had sections dealing with the health risks connected with tobacco, drugs, and alcohol. This oversight concerning suicide education should not be attributed to complete negligence on the part of the education departments. Our school systems are, in actuality, controlled by the people of the state. A majority of parents in the United States are fearful about the effects of smoking, drug usage, and drinking among their children. They see these as immediate problems. Unfortunately, many of these same parents either do not view youthful suicide as a major crisis or are afraid that instruction about it might invite participation.

Other parents do not want their children, even of high school age, exposed to the serious problems of life. Either they feel that the youngsters are too immature, or else the adults have a romantic nostalgia about the teen years and want their children to think only about innocuous events like dances and football games.

"Let them worry about that [suicide and other problems] when they're older," one mother said. "They should be enjoying life now."

Tragically, parents like the ones above do not realize that many American young people are committing suicide before this mysterious age when they will supposedly be able to handle such hard facts about life.

At other times the pressure against health instruction on the subject of suicide may come from within the school system. A member of the Department of Education of the State of Oregon confessed that the department was ". . . having a difficult time in getting educational administrators to face up to the 'real problems' of adolescence. Perhaps your book will give some assistance."

That state and others like it are to be commended for at least considering the inclusion of suicide in their curriculum. Ms. Frances A. Mays, Supervisor of Health and Physical Education for Virginia, wrote, "Our present health education curriculum guides do not include provisions for health education related to the problem of youthful suicide. This is something that will be taken into consideration when the guides are revised."

In Idaho, the state "Health Curriculum for Kindergarten Through Sixth Grade" contains extensive sections on how youngsters might develop greater self-esteem, more meaningful interpersonal relationships, and methods to deal with emotions. Mr. Rick Kearns, Health Consultant for the Idaho Department of Education, said, "I think you will find that if children could exhibit these qualities throughout life there would be much lower suicide rates." And right he is. The destruction of self-esteem and an inability to deal with self-destructive emotions are two major causes of youthful suicide.

New Jersey pupils "with emotional problems whether manifesting aggressive or withdrawal tendencies are identified, evaluated and programmed individually . . . Some are referred for professional services outside the domain of the school, while some are treated within the milieu of the school either individually or in small groups."

All these efforts are beneficial and hopeful. Perhaps as the public becomes more concerned about the rise in youthful suicides, state departments of education will be able to facilitate more direct programs in suicide prevention.

There is another area which also needs intensive research and public education: the effect of nutrition upon the emotions. Young people do tend to eat more junk food than adults. Therefore, a chemical imbalance may exist in their bodies. This can sometimes lead to severe depression. Dr. H. L. Newbold, author of *Mega-Nutrients and Your Nerves,* is a psychiatrist who discovered that he could do a great deal more for his patients through nutrition than he did psychologically. The treatment of mental depression and other mental health problems nutritionally is a big, challenging field and one which appears to offer assistance to some suicidal young people.

Other agencies offer aid to would-be suicides. Most large cities have consultation services. These clinics are staffed with trained mental health professionals. Frequently, there is no cost for the patient because the staff donates its time and services.

Also, as mentioned earlier there are over 200 suicide prevention centers in the United States, some of which do provide consultation services in addition to the immediate hotline assistance. A selected list is to be found at the end of this book. Most suicide or crisis prevention centers only offer temporary help because they realize the suicidal crisis is short-lived. Many times, if a person can be guided through the darkest moments, he or she will not commit suicide. For those people, whose hope is still strong enough for them to communicate with another person, the point of no return may never be reached if a center can intervene in time.

These centers are supported by private and public funds, such as The United Way, staffed with professionals, and generally use well-trained volunteers to handle the hotline calls. A few universities that offer courses in behavioral sciences maintain a crisis intervention center to assist people who are facing emotional stress and also to train the university students in actual field work.

In general, there are many avenues to help for a suicidal person. Support can come from a friend or relative or an outside organization. The next chapter will detail the workings of one such outside agency: The San Francisco Suicide Prevention Center.

9

February 10th—11:14 A.M.

San Francisco Suicide Prevention Center

Yesterday a young man leaped from the Golden Gate Bridge. Moments before he was a human being with hopes and dreams and much unhappiness. Now he is a statistic: the 591st suicide to end his life by jumping from the Golden Gate Bridge.

"San Francisco is the suicide capital of the United States," says Roger Cornut, the Executive Director of San Francisco Suicide Prevention, Inc.

Mr. Cornut, nattily dressed in a red and black striped tie and blue sports jacket, physically resembles Bob Hope. His conversation is sprinkled with glints of humor, flicked off in a French-Swiss accent. But there is no flippancy when he discusses the goals and projects of the Center. He leans forward, elbows propped on the desk top, leaving only inches between himself and the interviewer's tape recorder.

In body language, this announces, "What I'm talking about is important to me."

The help offered by the Center is a vital concern of every member of the Center whether he or she is on the paid staff or one of the 150 volunteers who handle the phones. If you are talking with Faith Testi, the Executive Secretary, or with Hazel Levitt, Director of Volunteers, everything stops when the phone rings. There is a silent moment or two while they reassure themselves that someone is dealing with the latest cry for help.

"We like to believe that there is something intrinsically good about helping someone who is hurting," says Roger.

No paper to be filed or letter to be answered is more important than providing aid at the very moment that assistance is desired. Everyone is trained to answer the telephone and does so on occasions when many calls come in at the same time. Only Roger does not speak with any callers for fear his accent may hinder the success of the conversation.

The Center receives many phone calls besides those from people who may be on the brink of suicide. The organization has two Drug Lines for either drug users or their parents and relatives to call if they have questions or emergencies. There is a Grief Counseling Program in which those who have suffered a loss by suicide or other traumatic circumstances may be guided through a period of stress by one of the volunteers or staff members. The Senior

Information Line, which is an extension of the San Francisco Commission on the Aging, is an information and referral line for the elderly. The Friendship Line is a service where specially trained volunteers regularly call elderly persons to offer emotional support.

Besides these direct, person-to-person services, San Francisco Suicide Prevention figures importantly in the education of people' and groups throughout the Bay Area. Staff members offer consultation, training, and seminars to schools, universities, hospitals, and mental health agencies. In 1976, more than 4000 students heard talks by representatives of the Center.

"Traditionally, suicide prevention centers are Caucasian businesses," Rogers admits. To prevent this from happening with the San Francisco Center, special staff members were hired to reach the minority groups in the city.

San Francisco has an official Chinese population of 64,000 though the actual figure may be closer to 100,000 as a result of illegal immigration. An Oriental-American social worker who spoke two Chinese dialects was sent by the Center to train Chinese mental health workers. The eighteen to twenty annual cases of suicide among the city's 100,000 blacks is higher than the national rate. Therefore, black consultants from the Center visited every black agency, church, or club in San Francisco to offer consultation and seminars about depression and self-destructive behavior. Whether it is for an individual or a group, the Center is willing to extend any help available.

From the Center's inception in 1963, help has been the key word for the organization. In that year a British BBC correspondent, Bernard Mayes, arrived in San Francisco to discover that the city with the highest suicide rate in the United States had no agency dealing directly with potential suicides. Mr. Mayes, a former minister, was familiar with the suicide prevention work of the Samaritans in England, so he had a phone installed in his room and released a few public announcements that he would take calls from those people undergoing an emotional crisis.

Within a few days, he was swamped with calls and realized this could not be a one-man operation. San Francisco Suicide Prevention soon moved into a basement with about six volunteers.

Slowly, over the years the organization has grown. Today, there are five full-time staff members, a number of part-time helpers, and approximately 150 volunteers. The headquarters are located on Geary Boulevard above a tattoo parlor. The second floor of the building, given over exclusively to the Center, has been subdivided into a network of offices and rooms.

This February morning, twenty-four hours after the bridge suicide, it is clear in San Francisco, and the temperature registers a mild seventy degrees. In the distance, the orange stanchions of the famous bridge protrude from a morning sea fog. Inside the

Center, the mood is calm but efficient as the offices echo with ticking typewriters and ringing phones.

Even the size and function of the rooms reflect the goals of the agency. The smallest office is the cubicle occupied by Roger Cornut. Roger confesses his room is stuffy, but if he opens the sliding window he has to endure the traffic noise. There are no fancy desks, carpeting, or wall paintings to emphasize the fact that this is the office of the Executive Director. But there is no need for such decorations. Roger Cornut is not on an ego trip; he is on a mission.

The same Spartan attitude is evident in the other business offices of the Center. The small room used by Faith Testi and Abby Goodman, who is the public relations person, is cramped, and each centimeter of space is economically employed.

Why?

The purpose of the salaried staff, according to Roger, is solely to organize and direct the volunteer program.

Appropriately, the two largest rooms are the meeting room, which is filled with folding chairs and a portable chalkboard, and the area that contains the suicide hotline phones.

The meeting room is used for staff conferences and most important, for the training sessions of the volunteers. When an adult calls or writes, indicating interest in acting as a volunteer, he or she is sent a form, which Roger describes as "almost a psychological test." After this is returned, the applicant comes in for the first interview with a staff member. If there seems to be no problem, such as immaturity or emotional difficulties, the person is assigned to the next bracket of training sessions.

The training period lasts for eight weeks, with one three-hour meeting per week. The instruction is handled by a team composed of a psychiatrist, social workers, a drug specialist, and other mental health professionals. The potential volunteers are given a basic background in suicidology, mental illness, the drug culture, and community resources. Role-playing is used to evaluate the students' maturity level and sensitivity to the problems of others. The Center has also accumulated a library of special recordings to help the volunteers learn how to handle callers and their individual problems. These educational devices are augmented by having the new volunteers come to the Center and listen to actual calls.

After the two-month training period is completed, there is a second interview for the applicant. At this time all the information available about the student is pooled. At least three staff members have had an opportunity to observe closely the new volunteer so the final filtering process is thorough. If the student passes this second interview, he or she is placed on a probationary period of answering the telephones under close supervision.

Who volunteers for this important work?

Roger says, "We're lucky to have many younger volunteers where there is more flexibility" than with some older people, who tend to be judgmental and preachy; needless to say, though, some older volunteers do remarkably well.

Many of the younger volunteers are considering the mental health field as a future profession and, having heard about the excellent training program of San Francisco Suicide Prevention, enroll to "try themselves" before making final decisions about their future.

Volunteer Director Hazel Levitt feels that people who have suffered their own hurts make excellent volunteers. She says "gay people are among the best." This is because they have been sensitized by life and not because the Center receives hundreds of phone calls each year from desperate homosexuals on the verge of suicide.

Two volunteers are handling the chores this morning in the heart of the Center, which is a large room with two desks and three telephones. Above one desk is a vibrantly-colored poster, which states that "Suicide Doesn't Have To Happen." Alongside the poster is a giant map of the city, divided into districts.

One phone is in use; the other mute for the moment. Leslie is speaking with a young woman who has been seized by indefinable fears and needed someone to speak with about these pervasive thoughts. While Leslie is guiding the woman by asking questions, the caller is unsuccessfully trying to learn Leslie's last name. Volunteers only reveal their first name to a caller.

The third phone, the light green instrument, is the Center's unlisted number. At all times the volunteers must have at their disposal a free outside line in case the need arises to call for emergency police or medical services. Last week this phone once again proved its worth. A person called, threatening suicide within minutes. A volunteer was able to send an ambulance and another volunteer to save the would-be suicide.

The other person on duty this morning, Peter, is checking through the library of books and periodicals dealing with suicide, as well as the Center's files containing its own research. Possibly motivated by yesterday's bridge suicide, a television reporter arrived earlier for an interview. He asked if it were true that no blacks have ever jumped from the Golden Gate Bridge. Peter feels that the Center's records will prove that there have been black suicides at that site and is trying to document the fact while Leslie helps the caller.

Leslie is a twenty-two-year-old pre-med student with a major in biology, philosophy, and psychology. She describes herself as "antisuicide and prolife." She first became interested in the suicide prevention center when she heard about the organization from another person. What appealed to her was that "you just ask people questions to help them ventilate their aggressions or their anger or their hostility. I thought that would be interesting because it would make me feel I wasn't the only one. In a way, it would be mutually therapeutic."

Leslie believes she has achieved this goal. The training and telephone experience have been highly instructive for her. "You learn how to approach your problem by questions. If you know how to clarify the problems with the caller, that can lead you to the right solution." And that's the premise of the Center's work. "We're not advice-givers. It's a sounding-board operation."

Having been with the Center for about a year and a half, Leslie follows a schedule that most volunteers observe. She works about twenty to twenty-four hours a month. A person may fill a four-hour slot, such as from nine in the morning until one in the afternoon, or occasionally may be asked to do an overnight stint: eleven P.M. to seven A.M.

Perhaps Leslie's most startling call was not a potential suicide but a bomber. The man bombed telephone booths in a protest against Nelson Rockefeller, who held stock in the telephone company. The bomber also viewed his actions as a movement against Fascism, believing the United States was Fascistic because the country supported organizations such as the CIA and FBI. The man chose to call the Center because he knew they would try to stop him. He wanted to ventilate his anger.

The phone rings, and Leslie immediately answers, speaking in a soft voice that conveys many emotions: empathy, open-mindedness, and concern about the caller's problem. After about fifteen minutes Leslie realizes that this caller seems to be the type that the Center terms manipulative.

A manipulative caller, in Leslie's estimation, is "someone who does everything in his or her power to tell you the same story over and over again. They try all different tactics to keep you on the phone for an hour or an hour and a half because basically they're lonely. They want someone to talk to."

Another type of call which the Center receives is from the "persistent caller." Some persistent callers have been phoning the Center for many years and may phone as many as fifty times in one night. The Center keeps a special list of these people along with the records maintained on every caller. This information is highly confidential.

The following is a sample phone call. The conversation is not real but simulated. The Prevention Center does not release any information to an outsider. Confidentiality is promised to anyone who phones, and that promise is strictly observed.

The telephone rings and Leslie answers. "San Francisco Suicide Prevention Center. This is Leslie. May I help you?"

A young-sounding man blurts out, "I think I'm going to kill myself."

Calmly, "Why?"

"Oh, God! I've got so many problems. I don't know what to do."

"Would you like to tell me about your problems?"

"Which one? I have so many."

Leslie is using the question technique while listening fully to what the person says. She does not interrupt. This is the reason why the person telephoned the Center; he needed someone to listen to him.

"I think I'm going to be fired from my job. Everyone is out at lunch now. I'm alone so that's why I called. I'm worried that someone might come in here and kill me."

Leslie does not point out the inconsistency of someone who wants to commit suicide being worried about being killed. "Why do you feel that you may be fired."

More information slowly comes out. The young man has angered his fellow employees by constantly playing tricks on them. Leslie helps him realize that such conduct might well convince someone to discharge him. She also leads the man to see that there is little danger that someone will enter the office and kill him merely to steal a typewriter. More problems emerge. The man is living at home but cannot get along with his parents. He must find his own apartment.

Suddenly the client's conversation jumps backward. "I'm going to get fired and won't have any money. What will I do?"

"We talked about that. What did you decide was the thing that would get you fired?"

"Playing tricks."

"Right."

"I won't do that any more."

Leslie asks, "Now is there anything else you want to talk about?"

Pause. "No. Can I call you again if I have to?"

"You can call me as often as you want."

"You're Leslie. You're my counselor, right?"

"No, I'm not a counselor. I'm just a friend. But

you can call me. I'm not likely to be here when you do call. But there's *always* someone here to help you."

"Okay."

"How are you feeling now?" Leslie asks.

"Okay."

"Good. Now get back to your work. And keep thinking about all the good things we've talked about."

In a real situation, of course, the phone conversation goes on longer. The volunteer would take time to investigate with the caller whether the person has been having recurring thoughts about suicide, what he or she has done about it in terms of developing inner strength, and in what ways those problems have affected his or her relationships with family and friends.

While Leslie is busy on the phone, Peter returns to be on hand if a second call should come while Leslie is still dealing with the first. He has located the Center's research files, which prove there have been black suicides from the Golden Gate Bridge.

If clothes reflect the inner person, Peter is a together person. His dark green turtleneck coordinates with his light green corduroys and green socks. His hair and beard are a shade lighter than his warm brown eyes. The eyes and voice are both soft and empathetic: a sincere quality impossible to manufacture.

Peter has been at the Center for only nine months, although he has been in the field for ten years. His first link with mental health work occurred when he was twelve years old and lived in Napa, California. A neighbor and close friend of the family was the superintendent of the Napa State Hospital. The man prevailed upon Peter's family to hire a patient as a part-time gardener and general handyman. This patient subsequently became a very good friend of Peter's and of his dad's.

Later Peter studied to become a psychologist, a profession he works in at present. His first field placement had been at a day treatment center that handled suicidal persons. One phone call he received while there stands out in his mind as "memorable."

A man was so distraught that he felt suicide was the only avenue of escape. Having experienced tremendous recent losses, among them the deterioration of his marriage, the patient had developed another alarming symptom. He found himself falling asleep and then waking up some time later miles away. He would be dressed in combat gear and carrying a weapon—and not quite sure how he got there.

Concerned about the man's suicidal tendencies, Peter invited him to the Day Treatment Center for a talk. Soon after, Peter was able to help the man find professional consultation to see him through his problems. In fact, Peter accompanied the man on the first visit.

When asked if the San Francisco Suicide Prevention Center received many calls from people who wanted to express their gratitude for the assistance they had received, Peter thought a moment.

"No. Not really. I guess more than you'd expect. But it would be nice if more people were that thoughtful."

The telephone rings, and Peter immediately lifts the receiver. Another person seeks help.

While Peter is speaking on the phone, Roger writes him a note, thanking him for finding the information about black suicides and the bridge. Roger is free for a few moments, but only a few moments. Being the Executive Director of a center is not a paper-pushing job. Other urgent matters await his attention. He is pleased, however, that the Center was able to find documentation for the television reporter.

The Golden Gate Bridge is a recurring theme that surfaces continually in conversations related to suicide. Minutes before, Peter had mentioned that one of the Center's own workers had stopped a suicide on the bridge. By sheer coincidence, David and his wife were taking a Sunday drive across the bridge.

His wife saw someone climbing up the railing. "David, something's happening."

Though the traffic was heavy, David managed to stop the car and knock the man down before he could jump.

But why this persistent preoccupation with the Golden Gate Bridge?

Roger feels there is "a magical attraction" about the bridge. Some people, when they are having problems, view it as *the* answer. "If things get worse, there's always the bridge," they tell themselves. Ironically, close to half the suicides drive across the Bay Bridge, which would be equally effective for their purposes, continue through the city, and then leap from the Golden Gate span.

There have been efforts by local groups, such as San Francisco Suicide Prevention, to have the bridge authority erect a barrier. So far these requests have been denied. If a solid wall were put up, this could endanger the bridge; the added structure would heighten the effect of lateral winds. To implant a system of single poles, which could be spaced so closely that no one could slip through the openings, would cost millions of dollars.

There is another reason why no plan has been set into motion to reduce the number of suicides from the Golden Gate Bridge. Many people in the city feel that if the attraction of the bridge is reduced, then suicidal people would simply seek other means. This attitude may change. When Roger came to the Center years ago, many people in the city did not even want to talk about suicide. Now there is public concern that is continually growing.

What lies ahead for the Center?

"We're not empire builders and don't want to spread needlessly," Roger explains. The Center is thinking ahead to a possible program of after-care for people who have been hospitalized following a suicide attempt. The three or four months after release from the hospital are important ones. The

Center would like to institute a program where volunteers could call these people and provide emotional support.

Now Roger has to be off to attend to his other duties. Leslie and Peter are replaced by the next scheduled volunteers. And the suicide hotline is ringing.

Modestly, and in a vast understatement, Roger Cornut sums up the Center's achievements. "We like to believe we've been a bit helpful."

10

After

The hours and days following a suicide attempt or a successful suicide are difficult ones for both the victim and the survivors. "Experience indicates that many survivors of apparently serious suicide attempts have decided that the attempt was a mistake. . . . This awareness comes quickly without external help," wrote James C. Diggory in *Suicidal Behaviors*.

The person who tried suicide reaches that realization in the initial recovery period for several reasons. First is the fact that all the problems that existed before the attempt are still there, but now the person has the added responsibility of regaining his or her physical health.

"I tried to kill myself once physically," said nineteen-year-old Jim H. "But I did it hundreds of times in my head afterwards. I had tried a razor blade. It was terrible waking up the next morning. I thought I would never wake up again. And there I was alive and with bloody wrists. For the next few nights I kept dreaming and kind of reliving the suicide. My wrists were bandaged, but as I rolled over in bed or pulled the blankets, all those long thin scabs would sting. And if I was asleep, I guess that stinging made me dream of the attempt. I'd wake up shivering. Not from the cold, because I wasn't cold. It was just the fear of what I had tried to do and pictured in my head that I was doing again and again."

If it's possible to say that any positive result comes from a suicide attempt, that benefit would be the aftereffect of shock. The first few hours are filled with unhappiness about the lack of success, and a numbness as well as a complete inability to handle any problem. As hard as it may be to believe, for some people even the simple procedure of making a cup of instant coffee is impossible to coordinate. Consider Jim's experience.

"I don't know what it was. I couldn't get it straight. Putting the pot of water on and getting the cups and spooning the coffee in. I didn't know what to do first. I just stood in the kitchen, staring at the cupboards and stove, wondering why I wasn't dead and how I could go on living."

These hours after the attempt, and possibly even the first few days, are the times when the victim should have strong emotional support, if not complete direction, from friends and relatives. Phone calls should be made for him or her and if any errands must be run, the person should be driven by someone. Of utmost importance is the fact that the people surrounding the person who attempted suicide act natural and speak of ordinary things so that the person realizes life *is* going to continue. The period of hysteria experienced by the victim is over and certainly should not be reintroduced by anyone else. Normal routines should be set into motion once again so the victim can begin to function.

But then comes the second mental stage for the person who attempted suicide. Sometimes the change in attitude comes from a realization of what that person almost accomplished. When someone is teetering on the brink of suicide, the thought processes are disorganized and blurred so that he or she may not really be fully conscious of the consequences of his or her actions. When the person begins to recover from the physical effects of the attempt, the cold hard fact strikes home. There may even be a complete inability to believe that he or she actually tried to end his or her life.

"I couldn't believe it," a high school girl said. "I mean . . . I had really tried to kill myself. It was kind of like looking back at another person. Not me. I wouldn't have done that. Never me. But I had."

This emotional jolt usually motivates the person to begin taking steps to rebuild his or her life. All the people interviewed for this book who had tried suicide admitted that they had made a mistake. Most, looking back, were frightened that they might have succeeded. And almost all the interviewees said that shortly after the attempt things began to improve. In truth, the situations started to clear up because the people did what they had not been doing prior to trying to commit suicide. They began to work actively to solve their problems. The route back was different for each of them. A few had suggestions to pass along to others so that their return might be easier.

"In general, stay away from emotional vacuousness. Express your feelings even if many people hate you for it. And—this for the young women especially—stay away from masks. A good reading of the novels of Jean Rhys will give you the specifics of what to avoid. Have close friends rather than acquaintances."

Another twenty-year-old girl, Barbara N., explained that shortly after the attempt, she knew that she had better receive professional help. She enrolled in a free clinic where she attended a private therapy session two times a week for the first few months and then had several more months of one meeting per week. She offered this advice about her experiences in accepting help from a professional in the field of mental health:

"If you're going to do it [seek professional help], then do it. If you're going to go through with it, then don't screw around. Don't go in like it's a game. Don't try to get a band-aid for your wound. Stay away from drugs. As far as I'm concerned, be very wary of a psychiatrist who's into pushing you with a lot of pills unless you're a chronic insomniac and have to get to sleep at night. But any doctor who's really into pushing pills and all kinds of mood alternators, whether it's to get you up or get you down, watch that. It's no good."

Most large cities have several clinics so the would-be patient will need to make evaluations about where he or she would like to receive help. Barbara explained her selection process.

"The reason why I went to the group that I went to was because I sensed that, for one thing, they're mostly people who are, if not my age, only a few years older, so they're very close to where I am. They weren't typical straight and narrow freaks. The guy [the therapist] wouldn't pass out if I said I had premarital sex, and he wouldn't pass out if I said I smoked pot. And he wouldn't try to tell me that was my problem. That's not my problem. Don't try to tell me that it is."

And what were Barbara's sessions like?

"They weren't very directive. He'd let me talk until he started to get a feel for what was going on, and then he'd start asking questions. Then he could come out with some kind of analysis of what I was going through. Also he was tough. He wouldn't let me sneak away from something that I didn't want to deal with. If it really was going to cause me pain and wouldn't do any good for me, then he'd stay away from that.

"He's very good. I have a lot of respect for him. I definitely do. He'd really pin me down. There were times when I didn't like him much for that. When I first started going, I was terrified. Every time I walked down the street to go to the building, I would think, 'Why don't you leave well enough alone.' I always went, though. I never copped out."

Carl P. found that having something to work toward in the future helped him to reenter normal living. The twenty-two-year-old man, with ambitions to be a writer, had tried suicide twice. Following the first attempt, he made no real effort to avoid another attempt. In fact, he truly thought that he was beyond suicide. The second try came only weeks after the first. That time was even more frightening for him because that's when he realized there might be a third or fourth until he finally succeeded.

"After the second attempt, I don't know if I picked up the pieces. But since then I've been working on two novels. Therefore, I have some stock in the future. Sometimes I still feel as though I am living in a vacuum. Sometimes I still feel doomed to live a totally pained and botched-up life. But mostly I have more hope than that. I couldn't tell you why, except that my projects have helped. Also I have had a few good friends since my last suicide attempt. I certainly wouldn't say that everything has been solved, though."

Most of those who had attempted suicide and consented to be interviewed seemed to have mellowed and accept the fact that every minute of their lives is not going to be gloriously happy. But now they have somehow found the strength within themselves to face the bad times. None of them believed that their action was a disgrace, although many persons who attempt suicide do experience that feeling. In contrast, the friends and especially the relatives of the failed or the successful suicide usually do consider the action disgraceful.

This belief can be injurious to all parties. If the person who attempted suicide has survived, reentry into a normal life will be even more difficult if he or she is made to feel a terrible deed has been committed. A terrible deed *was* committed, but not because of what other people may think. The tragedy is that a human life was almost lost. But there is nothing intrinsically shameful about a person's having become so overwrought that he or she saw no other way out.

For the family who are the survivors of successful suicides, especially young suicides, the first days and weeks are extremely rough. This is why organizations such as San Francisco Suicide Prevention, Inc., are instituting programs to counsel survivors. Many persons experience conflicting emotions toward the suicide victim. First, there is often the belief that disgrace has been brought down upon the family name. No matter how the problem is explained to some people, they will not view suicide any other way. Thus, many survivors feel rage toward the dead person. At the same time there are tremendous guilt feelings.

"Why didn't I know this was going to happen?"

"Could I have prevented the suicide?"

"Did I cause the suicide?"

The confusion, self-recrimination, and shame that most survivors of a successful suicide experience made it impossible for an actual interview to be in-

cluded in this text. Of the five different families contacted, none wished to speak to an outsider about
the suicide of their sons or daughters. Either they
were still sorting out their thoughts or they simply
did not want to reexamine the dreadful times.

James A. Wechsler, a writer for the New York
Post, discussed the effect of his son's suicide in a column on May 17, 1977. He and his wife had collabo-
rated on a book about the episode—*In a Darkness*—
the main message of which was, ". . . how often we
failed to say or do some things that might (or might
not) have mattered . . ."

The time immediately after an attempted or successful suicide is, indeed, hard on everyone. The relatives and friends of a successful suicide must find a
way to move beyond the sense of loss and assumed
guilt. Guilt implies a premeditated action. Rarely
have the survivors of a suicide purposely facilitated
that death. If anything, we *all* must share the blame
for poor communication and understanding among
each other. For, in truth, they are the immediate
causes of a suicide.

11

A Hard Look at Suicide

The prognosis is cloudy. Can we look forward to ever-rising suicide rates among young people? Or will the problem crest and then begin a downhill slide?

There are certain characteristics of our society which, unfortunately, might drive the statistics higher. Sociologists have been aware of the changing trends in the relationships within American families. Children quite often never see their grandparents. The nuclear family (mother, father and children) is becoming increasingly fractionalized. Therefore, the danger of children growing up without the benefit of emotional support and understanding will be greater. As already indicated, this can produce psychologically wounded individuals.

Another trend in our everyday lives may also contribute to this same effect. More and more women are moving into the work field. No one is condemning the fight for women's rights, but as additional young mothers find employment, leaving their small children either with sitters or in day-care centers, we may see more youngsters growing up with a feeling of rejection.

On the other hand, there are hopeful signs. The widening public awareness of the seriousness of the problem should be applauded. Ten years ago people rarely spoke or even thought about young persons killing themselves unless a dramatic event happened in their town or city. Now mental health experts are being interviewed on television talk shows, and magazine articles as well as books on the subject for the lay citizen can be found in libraries and stores.

A by-product of this public attention will, we hope, be an introduction of suicide-prevention classes in our public school systems. Drug education went that route, and there is no reason that suicide education cannot. Such an improvement in the health curriculum of the nation's schools will aid the would-be suicide by strengthening his or her defenses and also be an assistance to friends and relatives of suicidal people. Effective help can then be provided to those who are seeking aid to fight their emotional stress.

There are other things, however, that we can do to attack this public health menace. Some suggestions are general and rather hard to facilitate. Others are more specific and could be implemented if people's concern was great enough.

1. *Philosophical Change.* Cultural changes within a society are extremely difficult to manipulate. So even

though we know that the American view of success can contribute to the suicide rate, there is little direct action we can take to change that. As of now, most Americans still view material gain and certain visible achievements as the major goals in life. Therefore, those who are not able to accumulate as many of these may experience a sense of failure and an attack on their sense of competence. A helpful remedy might be to widen the number of life styles and performances that we now label as successful. Is the generous, witty person who has a low paying job less desirable than another person who is bringing home a much higher salary? We prevent suicide, claiming we wish to preserve life. Perhaps we should then view life's true achievements in the sense of continued individual development rather than financial gains.

This change in point of view, of course, cannot be mandated by law, but a shift in attitudes can be brought about through education. The presence of efforts to improve self-esteem and show the worth of every individual is an encouraging start by our educational systems.

2. *Support of Suicide Prevention Activities.* As shown, our crisis intervention centers do an excellent job. There is a continuing need, however, for additional mental health facilities. One reason that the urban black suicide rates are so high is that blacks tend to live in areas where there is a scarcity of clinics and health agencies. Public, state, and federal funds are now supporting many organizations that are fighting

the suicide problem. More money would mean a faster and more effective development of such resources.

3. *Establishment of Additional Programs.* There remains a lack of other approaches to the situation. For example, follow-up procedures in dealing with attempted suicides are still minimal. At present most people who have tried to commit suicide leave the hospital after a few days and generally receive no follow-up attention. Thus, the victim is left to his or her own devices in what could be a most crucial period.

Also, the family members of a successful suicide should be viewed as victims. They need guidance and emotional bolstering in the time immediately after the suicide. If not assisted, the survivor may become obsessed with the suicide for the remainder of his or her life. One psychiatrist wrote: "The suicide puts his (or her) skeleton in the survivor's psychological closet."

4. *Massive Public Education.* The country is on the move in this respect already, but the program could be widened and stepped up. If the average citizen is more thoroughly attuned to the danger signals of suicide, he or she can then become our first line of defense. With millions of people alert and watchful, suicide prevention would show far greater results.

This education can also take the form of classes for new parents. Hospitals now have such features to instruct both the mother and father in baby care. These workshops could broaden their scope and show their members how to care for the child's psychological needs. Most parents want to be the best parents they can. Often, the emotional injuries done to a growing youngster are unintentionally inflicted and are a result of a lack of awareness rather than a lack of love.

Today, youthful suicide is often an undiscussed threat to the resources of this country. And because this public health menace is still cloaked in silence by certain sectors of our society, intelligent, giving individuals who could lead useful, productive lives are dying at an early age. Our hope lies in the fact that efforts are being made to educate more people to the danger as well as to probe the causes of suicide in whatever segment of our society it occurs. These long-term projects, assisted by groups such as San Francisco Suicide Prevention, Inc., may in the long run prove equal to suicide's destruction of our young people. That is the goal toward which many are now working.

A Selected List of Suicide Prevention Centers

ALABAMA

Crisis Center of Jefferson County, Inc.
3600-8th Avenue, South
Birmingham, Alabama 35222

(205) 323-7777

North Central Alabama Crisis Call Center
P.O. Box 637
Highway 31 South
Decatur, Alabama 35601

(205) 355-8000

CALIFORNIA

Help Line, Inc.
P.O. Box 5658
China Lake, California 93555

(714) 446-5531

Suicide Prevention Center & the Inst. for Studies of Self-Destructive Behaviors
1041 S. Menlo Avenue
Los Angeles, California 90006

(213) 381-5111

*North Bay Suicide
Prevention, Inc.*
P.O. Box 2444
Napa, California 94558

(707) 643-2555 (Vallejo)
(707) 255-2555 (Napa)

Desert Hospital
P.O. Box 1627
Palm Springs, California
92262

(714) 346-9502

Help Center
5069 College Avenue
San Diego, California
92115

(714) 582-HELP

*San Francisco Suicide
Prevention, Inc.*
3940 Geary Blvd.
San Francisco, California
94118

(415) 221-1423

*Contra Costa Crisis Suicide
Intervention Center*
P.O. Box 4852
Walnut Creek, California
94596

(415) 939-3232

COLORADO

Suicide and Crisis Control
2459 South Ash
Denver, Colorado 80222

(303) 756-8485; 757-0988;
789-3073

*Crisis Center and Suicide
Prevention Service*
599 Thirty Road
Grand Junction, Colorado
81501

(303) 242-0577

*Pueblo Suicide Prevention
Center*
212 W. 12th Street
Room 122
Pueblo, Colorado 81003

(303) 545-9990

CONNECTICUT

*Greater Bridgeport Community
Mental Health Center*
1635 Central Avenue
Bridgeport, Connecticut
06610

(203) 384-1711

DELAWARE

Psychiatric Emergency Service
Sussex County Community
Mental Health Center
Beebe Hospital of Sussex
County, Inc.
Lewes, Delaware 19958

(302) 856-6626

Psychiatric Emergency Service
So. New Castle
Community Mental
Health Center
14 Central Avenue
New Castle, Delaware
19720

(302) 421-6711

DISTRICT OF
COLUMBIA

*Emergency Mental Health
Services*
1905 E Street, S.W.
Bldg. #25
Washington, D. C. 20003

(202) 629-5222

FLORIDA

Central Crisis Center
2218 Park Street
P.O. Box 6393
Jacksonville, Florida 32204

(904) 384-2234

*Crisis and Suicide
Intervention Service*
Brevard County Mental
Health Center, Inc.
1770 Cedar Street
Rockledge, Florida 32955

(305) 784-2433

*Crisis Intervention
of Sarasota, Inc.*
1650 S. Osprey Avenue
Sarasota, Florida 33578

(813) 959-6686

GEORGIA

*Fulton County Emergency
Mental Health Service*
99 Butler Street, S.E.
Atlanta, Georgia 30303

(404) 572-2626

*Carroll Crisis
Intervention Center*
201 Presbyterian Avenue
Carrollton, Georgia 30117

(404) 834-3326; 834-3327

Helpline
1512 Bull Street
Savannah, Georgia 31401

(912) 232-3383

HAWAII

Suicide and Crisis Center
200 N. Vineyard Blvd.
Room 603
Honolulu, Hawaii 96817

(808) 521-4555

ILLINOIS

Call for Help—
and Crisis Inter-Service, Inc.
7812 W. Main Street
Belleville, Illinois 62223

(618) 397-0963

Crisis Intervention and
Suicide Prevention Program
4200 North Oak Park
Avenue
Chicago, Illinois 60634

(312) 794-3609

Suicide Prevention Service
520 South 4th Street
Quincey, Illinois 62301

(217) 222-1166

INDIANA

Crisis & Suicide Intervention
Service in Marion County
Association
1433 N. Meridian Street
Indianapolis, Indiana
46202

(317) 632-7575

IOWA

Lee County Mental Health
Center
1013 Concert Street
Keokuk, Iowa 52632

(319) 524-3873

KANSAS

Wyandot Mental Health
Center
36th and Eaton Avenue
Kansas City, Kansas 66103

(913) 831-1773

Can Help
P.O. Box 1364
Topeka, Kansas 66601

(913) 235-3434; 235-3435

Suicide Prevention Service
3620 E. Sunnybrook
Wichita, Kansas 67210

(316) 686-7465

Bath-Brunswick Area Rescue, Inc.
159 Main Street
Brunswick, Maine 04011

(207) 443-3300

LOUISIANA

Baton Rouge Crisis Intervention Center, Inc.
THE PHONE
LSU Student Health Bldg.
Baton Rouge, Louisiana 70803

(504) 388-8222; 388-1234

Rescue, Incorporated
331 Cumberland Avenue
Portland, Maine 04101

(207) 774-2767

MARYLAND

The Rymland M.H.C.
Sinai Hospital of Baltimore, Inc.
Belvedere Avenue at Greenspring
Baltimore, Maryland 21215

(301) 367-7800, Ext. 8841

Crisis Line
1528 Jackson Avenue
New Orleans, Louisiana 70130

(504) 523-COPE

MAINE

Dial Help,
The Counseling Center
43 Illinois Avenue
Bangor, Maine 04401

(207) 947-6143 or
1-800-432-7810

MASSACHUSETTS

Rescue, Inc.
115 Southampton Street
Boston, Massachusetts 02118

(617) 426-6600

Samaritans
355 Boylston Street
Boston, Massachusetts
02116

(617) 247-0220

Ypsilanti Area Community Services
210 W. Michigan Avenue
Ypsilanti, Michigan 48197

(313) 485-0440

MICHIGAN

Suicide Prevention Center
1151 Taylor Avenue
Detroit, Michigan 48202

(313) 875-5466

Ottawa County Crisis Intervention Service
Help-Line
1111 Fulton Street
Grand Haven, Michigan
49417

(616) 842-4357

Crisis Clinic—Six Area Community Mental Health
1619 Fort Street
Lincoln Park, Michigan
48146

(313) 383-9000

MINNESOTA

Crisis Intervention Center
Hennepin County Medical
Center
701 Park Avenue, So.
Minneapolis, Minnesota
55415

(612) 347-2222; 347-3161

Emergency Social Service
100 So. Robert Street
St. Paul, Minnesota 55107

(612) 225-1515

MISSISSIPPI

Listening Post
P.O. Box 2072
Meridian, Mississippi
39301

(601) 693-1001

MISSOURI

*St. Francis Community
Mental Health Center*
St. Francis Drive at
Gordonville Rd.
Cape Girardeau, Missouri
63701

(314) 334-6400

*Western Missouri
Mental Health Center
Suicide Prevention Center*
600 East 22nd Street
Kansas City, Missouri
64108

(816) 471-3939; 471-3940

*Suicide/Crisis
Intervention Service
Life Crisis Services, Inc.*
7438 Forsyth
St. Louis, Missouri 63105

(314) 868-6300

MONTANA

Blackfeet Crisis Center
Blackfeet Reservation
Browning, Montana 59417

(406) 338-5525; 226-4291

Great Falls Crisis Center
Box 124
Great Falls, Montana 59401

(406) 453-6511

NEVADA

*Suicide Prevention
& Crisis Call Center*
Room 206, Mack SS
Building
University of Nevada
Reno, Nevada 89507

(702) 323-6111

NEW HAMPSHIRE

*North County Community
Services, Inc.*
330 School Street
Berlin, New Hampshire
03570

(603) 752-7404

*Central New Hampshire
Community
Mental Health Services, Inc.*
#5 Market Lane
Concord, New Hampshire
03301

(603) 228-1551

NEW JERSEY

Ancora Psychiatric Hospital
*Ancora Suicide Prevention
Service*
Hammonton, New Jersey
08037

(609) 561-1234

*Middlesex County–
Crisis Intervention*
37 Oakwood Avenue
Metuchen, New Jersey
08840

(201) 549-6000

*C.R.I. (Crisis,
Referral and Information)*
232 E. Front Street
Plainfield, New Jersey
07060

(201) 561-4800

NEW MEXICO

*Suicide Prevention
and Crisis Center, Inc.*
P.O. Box 4511, Sta. A
Albuquerque, New Mexico
87106

(505) 265-7557

The Crisis Center
Box 3563
University Park Br.
Las Cruces, New Mexico
88001

(505) 524-9241

NEW YORK

Refer Switchboard
214 Lark Street
Albany, New York 12210

(518) 434-1202

*Lifeline (Formerly Suicide
Prevention Service)*
Nassau County Medical
Center
2201 Hempstead Turnpike
East Meadow, New York
11554

(516) 538-3111

*National Save-A-Life
League, Inc.*
815 2nd Avenue
New York, New York
10017

(212) 736-6191

Suicide Prevention Service
29 Sterling Avenue
White Plains, New York
10606

(914) 949-0121

NORTH CAROLINA

Hassle House
1022 Urban Avenue
Durham, N. Carolina
27701

(919) 688-4353

Crisis Control Center, Inc.
P.O. Box 735
Greensboro, N. Carolina
27402

(919) 275-2852

*Crisis and Suicide
Intervention*
P.O. Box Q
Sanford, N. Carolina 27330

(919) 776-5431

NORTH DAKOTA

*Suicide Prevention
and Emergency Service*
9th and Thayer
Bismarck, N. Dakota 58501

(701) 255-4124

*Suicide Prevention
and Mental Health Center*
700 First Avenue, South
Fargo, N. Dakota 58102

(701) 232-4357

*Center for Human
Development*
509 South Third Street
Grand Forks, N. Dakota
58201

(701) 775-0525

OHIO

Support, Inc.
1361 W. Market Street
Akron, Ohio 44313

(216) 434-9144

*Crisis Intervention Center,
Inc.*
1341 Market Avenue, N.
Canton, Ohio 44714

(216) 452-6000

Suicide Prevention
1515 E. Broad Street
Columbus, Ohio 43215

(614) 221-5451; 221-5445

Rescue Crisis Services
One Stranahan Square
c/o United Central Service
Toledo, Ohio 43624

(419) 244-3063

OREGON

Crisis Service
127- N.A. Sixth Street
Corvallis, Oregon 97330

(503) 752-7030

University of Oregon
Crisis Center
Erb Memorial Union, Univ.
of Oregon
Eugene, Oregon 97403

(503) 686-4488

PENNSYLVANIA

Lifeline
520 E. Broad Street
Bethlehem, Pennsylvania
18018

(215) 691-0660

Philadelphia Suicide
Prevention Center
Room 430, City Hall
Annex
Philadelphia, Pennsylvania
19107

(215) 686-4420

SOUTH CAROLINA

Crisis Intervention Service
Greenville Area Mental
Health Center
715 Grove Road
Greenville, So. Carolina
29605

(803) 271-0220

TENNESSEE

Crisis Intervention Service
Helen Ross McNabb
Center
1520 Cherokee Trail
Knoxville, Tennessee
37920

(615) 637-9711

Suicide Crisis and
Intervention Service
P.O. Box 4068
Memphis, Tennessee
38104

(901) 726-5531, -5532, -
5534

Crisis Intervention Center
2311 Elliston Place
Nashville, Tennessee 37203

(615) 244-7444

TEXAS

*Suicide Prevention
of Dallas, Inc.*
P.O. Box 19651
Dallas, Texas 75219

(214) 521-5531

Crisis Intervention Center
730 E. Yandell
El Paso, Texas 79902

(915) 779-1800

*San Antonio Suicide
Prevention Center*
P.O. Box 10192
San Antonio, Texas 78210

(512) 734-5726 & 735-8328

Concern
P.O. Box 1945
Wichita Falls, Texas 76301

(817) 723-0821 or 0822

UTAH

Crisis Intervention Services
Granite Community Mental
Health Center
156 East Westminster
Avenue
Salt Lake City, Utah 84115

(801) 484-8761

WASHINGTON

*Crisis Clinic of
Thurston & Mason Counties*
P.O. Box 2463
Olympia, Washington
98507

Thurston County—(206)
352-2211
Mason County—(206) 426-
3311

Crisis Services
Community Mental Health
Center
107 Division Street
Spokane, Washington
99202

(509) 838-4651

WEST VIRGINIA

Contact—Huntington
520–11th Street
Huntington, W. Virginia
25705

(304) 523-3448

WISCONSIN

*Emergency Services—
Dane County Mental Health
Center*
31 So. Henry Street
Madison, Wisconsin 53703

(608) 251-2345

Milwaukee County
Mental Health Center
Psychiatric Emergency
Services
8700 W. Wisconsin Avenue
Milwaukee, Wisconsin
53226

(414) 257-5989

WYOMING

Help Line, Inc.
Cheyenne, Wyoming 82001

(307) 634-4469

A Selected Bibliography

A. Books

Alvarez, A. *The Savage God.* New York: Random House, 1972.

Farber, Maurice L. *Theory of Suicide.* New York: Funk & Wagnalls, 1968.

Farberow, Norman L., ed. *Suicide in Different Cultures.* Baltimore: University Park Press, 1975.

Hendin, Herbert. *The Age of Sensation.* New York: W. W. Norton & Co., Inc., 1975.

———. *Black Suicide.* New York: Basic Books, Inc., 1969.

Hyde, Margaret O. *Hot Line!* New York: McGraw Hill, 1974.

Klagsbrun, Francine. *Too Young to Die.* Boston: Houghton Mifflin Co., 1976.

McCormick, Donald. *The Unseen Killer.* London: Frederick Muller Limited., 1964.

Perlin, Seymour, ed. *A Handbook for the Study of Suicide.* New York: Oxford University Press, 1975.

Resnik, H. L. P., ed. *Suicidal Behaviors*. Boston: Little, Brown and Company, 1968.

Reynolds, David K., and Farberow, Norman L. *Suicide: Inside and Out*. Berkeley: University of California Press, 1976.

Savage, Mary. *Addicted to Suicide*. Berkeley: Bookpeople, 1975.

Wallace, Samuel E. *After Suicide*. New York: John Wiley & Sons, 1973.

Wechsler, James A. *In a Darkness*. New York: W. W. Norton & Co., Inc., 1972.

B. Periodicals

"Adolescent Suicide: the mass media and the educator." *Adolescence* 10:241–6, Summer 1975.

"Adolescent Suicide at an Indian Reservation." *American Journal of Orthopsychiatry* 44:43–9, January 1974.

"American Indian Suicide." *Psychiatry* 38:86–91, Fall 1975.

"Chico's Last Act." *Newsweek* 89:25–6, February 7, 1977.

"Communication of Suicidal Intent." *American Journal of Psychiatry* 115:724, 1959.

"Freddie Prinze: too much too soon." *Time* 190:37, February 7, 1977.

"Fort Suicide?" *Newsweek* 88:36, September 27, 1976.

"How to Prevent Suicide." *Ebony* 32:128–30, December, 1976.

"Parent-child Role Reversal and Suicidal States in Adolescence." *Adolescence* 9:365–70, Fall 1974.

"Public Health Approach to Suicide Prevention." *American Journal of Public Health* 65:144–7, February 1975.

"Steps to Suicide." *Science Digest* 78:24, September 1975.

"Suicide in Relation to Time of Day and Day of Week." *American Journal of Nursing* 75:263, February 1975.

"Suicide: let's separate fact from fiction." *Better Homes and Gardens* 55:66+, April 1977.

"Suicide: vulnerability of youth." *MH,* Summer 1975.

"Teen Suicide." *Ladies Home Journal* 94:68+, February 1977.

"Young Suicides." *Harper's Bazaar* 109:68–9, June 1976.

C. Pamphlets

Fawcett, Jan, M.D. *Before It's Too Late.* The American Association of Suicidology.

Frederick, Calvin J., and Lague, Louise. *Dealing with the Crisis of Suicide.* New York: Public Affairs Pamphlets, 1972.

Seiden, Richard H. *Public Affairs Report: Suicide: Preventable Death.* Berkeley: University of California, Vol. 15 No. 4, August 1974.

Resnick, H. L. P., ed. *Suicide Prevention in the '70s.* Rockville, Maryland: National Institute of Mental Health, 1973.

D. Organizations and Sources of Information

American Association of Suicidology
Box 3264
Houston, Tx. 77001

National Institute of Mental Health
Mental Health Emergencies Section
5600 Fishers Lane
Rockville, Md. 20852

Public Affairs Pamphlets
381 Park Avenue, South
New York, N.Y. 10016

Public Affairs Report
Institute of Governmental Studies
University of California
Berkeley, Ca. 94720

Index